BLACK MIKE

A WESTERN DUO

BLACK MIKE

A WESTERN DUO

WAYNE D. OVERHOLSER

ISBN 978-1-5047-8687-4
1 3 5 7 9 10 8 6 4 2

CIP data for this book is available from the Library of Congress

Blackstone Publishing
31 Mistletoe Rd.
Ashland, OR 97520

www.BlackstonePublishing.com

GUN IN HIS HAND

I

It was in the shank end of the afternoon when the train clattered to a stop in Ogallala and Dane Coe, hot and tired, stepped down from the rear day coach, war bag in one hand, a sacked saddle in the other. He was hot and sleepy and short-tempered. He hated trains just as he hated anything that tied him down or penned him in, and the roundabout trip from Butte had been tedious and tiresome.

Dane stood motionlessly for a moment, eyes searching the crowd for his brother Fred, but there was no sign of him. Irritated, he crossed the cinders to the depot, wishing he'd ridden south on his horse. He had taken the train only because he'd thought it would save time, for his father's letter had held a note of frantic urgency. He had written back, saying when he'd be in Ogallala, he'd settled his affairs, and he'd taken the first train.

Dane shouldered through the crowd, irritation growing in him. Now there was nothing to do but take the stage, and he disliked stages as much as he did trains. He was so bound up in his thinking that he did not notice the two men who had fallen in behind him. It was not until they were past the depot and moving up Main Street that the tall man said: "Howdy, Dane."

Dane looked at one, and then the other. The tall man was Ed Lanning, ramrod of the S Star that lay to the east of Dane's father's little BC. The other was a stranger, a small man with red splotches on his face and a heavy mustache that drooped down over the corners of a thin-lipped mouth. They moved up so that Dane was between them.

"Howdy, Ed," Dane said. "You the welcoming committee?"

"Sort of. Dane, this is Frank Ashton. I reckon you've heard of him."

"Howdy, Ashton." Dane gave the man a nod, masking his face against the surprise that rushed through him. This was big trouble, or Ashton wouldn't be here. "Yeah, I've heard of him, Ed. I've heard of Billy the Kid, too."

"Billy the Kid," Ashton snorted. "Just a fake who got some publicity. Afore I'm done, I'll make every damned reporter in the country forget Billy the Kid."

"You're in fine company, Ed," Dane said.

"I know," Lanning agreed. "Sam's idea, not mine."

Sam Drew was Lanning's boss, a burly man in whom ambition was a never-dying flame and to whom respectability was a fetish. It struck Dane as being peculiar that he'd sign on a killer like Frank Ashton.

"You're damned right I'm fine company," Ashton said as if uncertain how to take Dane's words. "For my money a star-toter ain't so much, not even if he has got a big name."

"In here," Lanning said. "Let's have a drink."

They pushed through the batwings of a saloon, Lanning ahead, Ashton in the rear. Dane put his war bag and saddle down and bellied up to the mahogany, Lanning on one side, Ashton on the other. Turning, Dane pinned his eyes on Ashton. He was young. The mustache, Dane thought, had been grown to give him the appearance of age, but actually it gave his narrow face a comical look.

Ashton returned Dane's stare. His eyes were pale blue, so pale they seemed entirely colorless. He asked: "Well, what do you see?"

"Not much." Dane took his drink and, putting the glass down, wiped his mouth with the back of his hand. "Thanks, Ed. I'll be moseying along. Got to see when the stage leaves town."

"I don't like what I just heard," Ashton said. "When you look at me, you're looking at a hell of a lot."

"Shut up, Frank," Lanning said testily. "I didn't fetch you along to gab. That's my job."

"Then get at it," Ashton said. "I ain't taking nothing off of this hairpin. Maybe he's big up there in Montana, but down here he's just a saddle bum who ain't even got a horse to put the saddle on."

Dane turned to him again, eyes dropping to the low-hung .45 on Ashton's right thigh. He raised his eyes to the man's face. "You pretty fast with that iron, friend?"

"Fast enough to smoke you down." Ashton sucked in a quick breath, eyelids drooping almost shut. "Want to find out?"

"Damn you, Frank!" Lanning shouted. "Shut up or get out of here!"

Dane gave Ashton his back. "You know, Ed, I've met up with a lot of fellows like him. Let 'em have a little luck and they're big as all hell."

Lanning motioned to the batwings. "Get out of here, Frank. I'll handle this."

Ashton hesitated, his lips trembling under his bushy mustache. Then he wheeled and stalked out. When the batwings slapped shut behind him, Dane said: "Four years can change a lot of things, Ed, but I never thought I'd see you with a coyote like that."

"I ain't proud. It's Sam's idea, like I told you." Lanning helped himself to another drink, frowning. "Four years things change, all right, and I don't like none of the changes."

Dane said nothing. He stood waiting, watching Lanning who was staring morosely at his empty glass. The S Star ramrod was a lanky, big-boned man, half a head taller than Dane who stood an even six feet. Now Lanning turned his gray eyes to Dane. He said: "Ashton wants to burn you down just to put another notch on his gun. I never believed there was men like him, but, damn it, he's really that way. He's fast and he's mean."

"You ain't scaring me," Dane said, "if that's what you're working at."

"I just wanted you to know." Lanning filled his glass again and let it stand. "Seems to me you was twenty-one when you left, and that was four years ago. That's right, ain't it?" Dane nodded, and Lanning went on: "You've made quite a name for yourself in them four years. The talk's come back from Montana."

"About these changes," Dane said irritably. "The Frenchman's still there, I reckon."

"Still there, muddy and lazy as ever." Lanning cleared his throat. "What are your plans, Dane?"

Dane had always liked Lanning, and he had always disliked Sam Drew. He'd been young when he'd left the country, too young to judge most men accurately, but he was sure he had been right about Drew. It was all right for a man to be ambitious, but not in the way Drew was, for he possessed the pressing kind of ambition that made him destroy anyone who stood in his way.

"I'm going home," Dane said finally. "Dad wrote like he was having trouble."

"He is, but you can't help him, Dane. You know how Sam is. He's got to have everything his way."

Dane was silent, thinking of Drew's foster daughter, Becky Burke. She'd been sixteen when he'd left, but at sixteen she'd been old enough to know that she was in love with Dane, and Dane had felt the same way about her. If he lived to be a thousand years old, he'd never forget the time he'd gone to Drew and asked permission to marry Becky.

It hadn't been enough for Drew to say no. He'd stood there in the living room of the S Star ranch house like an inflated toad, his wide face was dark as midnight, and he'd laid his tongue on Dane like a down-swinging axe handle. When Becky got married,

Sam Drew had said, she'd marry somebody, not the son of a psalm-singing visionary who didn't own a pot to cook a jackrabbit in.

There had been more, a lot more that Dane had tried to forget. He had left the country the next day, swearing to come back and show Sam Drew he was somebody. Well, he was back with a .44 on his hip, a reputation, and $52 in his pocket.

Dane poured another drink, and gulped it. He said bitterly: "I ain't forgot how Sam is, but I aim to help Dad regardless."

"You can't." Lanning shook his head. "I used to figure Bill Coe was just talk, but he's been hanging on, come hell or high water. If you go back, he'll keep hanging on, and you'll both get killed. If you don't, he'll sell out and things will be all right."

Bill Coe was mostly talk. Dane had known that since he'd been a boy. It was his mother who had the courage, the solid kind of courage that was like an anchor holding a ship in a high wind. Dane remembered the drifting years, remembered coming here to western Nebraska and his mother saying this was their home. They'd stay, regardless of what happened, and he remembered his brother Fred saying the day Dane had left the country: "You're running out, Dane. We need you, and we'll always need you."

"Let's lay this out where we can see it, Ed," Dane said. "You don't want me to go home. That it?"

Lanning cuffed back his Stetson and scratched the bald spot above his forehead. "That's it. Sam sent me and Ashton to see that you didn't come back. We're supposed to put you on the next train. It leaves at midnight."

"That'll be quite a chore," Dane said softly.

Lanning stared down at the polished bar top. "I know. I told you I didn't like it. You and me always got along, Dane, but, damn it, it's better for everybody if you take that train."

"This on account of Becky?"

Lanning shook his head. "Sam's got other plans for her."

"She ain't married?"

"No. This is something else, Dane. Maybe your dad wrote about the railroad. They've got steel laid almost to Prairie City and the grade finished plumb to your dad's place. Sam figures it'll make him rich. Settlers are coming in. They'll have a county and Sam allows that Prairie City will be the county seat."

"What's that got to do with me?"

Lanning shifted uneasily. "Your dad's giving Sam trouble. Got a town site staked out he calls Coeburg. The present plan calls for it being the end of steel."

It was plain enough then. Drew's Prairie City wouldn't be any more than a collection of sod houses if the railroad built on through it. There had been talk of a new county even before Dane had left home. Now, if the grangers were moving in, they'd be able to organize the county, and Bill Coe's place was centrally located so that it would have a geographical advantage over Drew's town.

"Looks like Sam's afraid of me," Dane said.

"He's just playing it safe. Bill's made some wild talk about what you'll do, but one man just ain't enough, Dane."

Dane shrugged. "It's my hide."

"It'll mean some more hides. Mine, maybe."

"You aiming to make me take that train?"

"I've got to try," Lanning said doggedly.

"I'll think about it," Dane said. "Now I'm gonna get me a room and sleep. I never could sleep in one of them damned coaches." He picked up his saddle and war bag. "Thanks, Ed."

He went out, leaving Lanning staring worriedly after him. He stopped in front of the saloon, looking along the street. Frank Ashton would not be far away. The sun was well down in the west now, throwing a bright glare upon the silver-colored dust of the street.

He thought absently that Ogallala was not the town it once was when it had been crowded with Texas cowhands and a dozen herds had been held on the other side of the South Platte waiting to be shipped. Ogallala had become a farmers' town, and that was the way it would be on the Frenchman. Sam Drew had recognized that.

Ashton appeared from a doorway along the street. He came toward Dane, swaggering a little, trying to make up for his youth and lack of size by bravado. Dangerous, all right, as dangerous as an undersize rattlesnake, and about as pleasant of appearance.

"Get your walking papers, tin star?" Ashton asked.

Dane had put down his saddle and war bag. He said—"Sort of."—and, reaching for tobacco and paper, rolled a smoke.

Ashton laughed, a taunting sound that ripped the control from Dane's smoldering temper. "I figured you'd take Ed's advice. Back in your own bailiwick you'd be tough as hell, but down here you ain't got a piece of tin to hide behind."

Dane fished a match out of his vest pocket. "I kind of miss it," he said easily. He took a step toward Ashton, snapping the match into flame with his thumbnail and firing his cigarette. Then he took one more step, a long one that brought him close to Ashton, and his fist swung upward. Ashton clawed for his gun, cursing shrilly, but he was too slow. Dane's blow caught him just below the mustache, knocked a tooth loose, and sent him crashing off the boardwalk.

Ashton came up to his feet, spitting blood, and this time got his Colt clear of leather, but the blow had stunned him enough to slow his draw, and again he was too late. A second blow battered him back into the dust. He lay motionlessly, staring at Dane in the strained way of a man who lacks the control of his body that it takes to bring him to his feet.

Stooping, Dane picked up Ashton's dropped Colt and threw it over the false front of the saloon. He said—"You ain't gonna live long, sonny."—and turned to Ed Lanning who was watching from the batwings. "Take the kid home, Ed. He's too young to be away from his mama."

Dane picked up his war bag and saddle and pushed through the gathering crowd. *A hell of a homecoming*, he thought, and wondered why his brother Fred hadn't met him …

II

The hotel was across the street at the end of the block. Dane signed the register and, glancing around the lobby, saw that it was almost deserted. Just two people—a girl in the corner who was reading a newspaper and a drummer who sat near the door idly smoking a cigar. Dane picked up his saddle and war bag, thinking there was something about the girl that reminded him of Becky, but he couldn't be sure, for she was holding the newspaper in front of her face.

Shrugging, he went up the stairs to his room. He was getting jumpy, he thought. Actually he hadn't been able to see enough of the girl to know whether she looked like Becky or not. It was just that he wanted to see Becky, to find out why she hadn't married, and what Sam Drew's plans for her were. But to think she'd actually be here was foolish. The S Star lay eighty miles to the south, and as far as he knew there was no reason for her to be in Ogallala. Not to see him, anyhow.

Dane dropped his war bag and saddle in the corner and moved to the window. For a long time he stood staring into the street, thinking of his father's dreams and of Fred who was much like their father, and how his mother had somehow made them stay on their place just north of the Frenchman. He thought of the four years since he had left and of the money he had sent home. He felt a quick pang of regret. Then it was gone. Even if he had saved the money, it would not have been enough to make Sam Drew admit Dane was a success.

It was dusk now, and lamps were blooming along the street, throwing yellow fingers of light into the wide dust strip. Dane went down the stairs to the lobby. The girl was still in the chair, the newspaper in front of her face. *Funny,* he thought. *She could have it memorized by now.*

Dane stopped at the desk, asking: "When does the stage leave for the Frenchman country?"

"Six in the morning," the clerk said. "You can get breakfast in the dining room before it goes."

"Thanks," Dane said, and stepped through the archway into the dining room.

When he finished his meal, he scooted his chair back and rose. Lanning was waiting in the archway, his bony face very somber. When Dane came up, he said: "Ashton didn't like what you done to him."

"I didn't think he would. Keep him out of my way, Ed."

"You're pegging him wrong. I told you he's fast with his cutter, and he's ornery as hell."

Dane swore. "Damn it, Ed. I don't scare easy. I've been up against some boys who were really ornery. This Ashton is just a kid who thinks he's tough because he's got a gun and a mustache."

Dane would have pushed past Lanning if the S Star ramrod had not blocked his way. "Wait a minute, Dane. Ashton says Becky's in town. I ain't seen her and maybe he's lying, although I don't know why he would. Anyhow, it struck me that maybe you'd got word to her to meet you here."

"No, I didn't do anything of the kind."

Lanning gave a small nod as if relieved. "I'll take your word for it. Now are you gonna be on that train?"

"No. You still aiming to put me on?"

"The answer's the same. I've got to try."

"I'd hate like hell to kill you, Ed."

"I'd hate it, too."

"Why are you working for Drew, Ed?"

Lanning stepped out of the archway.

"You wouldn't believe me if I told you, and at half past eleven me and Ashton are coming up to your room. I'm hoping you'll change your mind before then."

"Don't count on it," Dane said, and moved through the archway past Lanning.

What had been a crazy possibility, that the girl in the lobby was Becky now became a probability, but as he moved toward the stairs, he saw that she was gone. He went to his room, the heaviness a disappointment in him. There was no telling now where she was. For four years he had tried to put Becky out of his mind, but he had never entirely succeeded. He had often wondered if she were married, but his folks had never mentioned her in their letters and he had never been able to bring himself to ask.

It was completely dark in the hall except for the single bracket lamp above the stairs. Dane put a hand on his gun, thinking that Ashton was the kind who would shoot him in the back if he had a chance. He paused outside his room, listening and hearing nothing, then he turned the knob and threw the door open. He slid into the room, moving fast so that he was silhouetted for only a moment against the thin hall light.

"How are you, Dane?" a voice said.

Dane pulled his gun instinctively, and his finger was hard on the trigger before he realized that the voice was Becky Burke's. He leaned against the wall, breathing hard, his eyes on the girl's slim figure. She was standing by the window, facing him, the light from the street framing her straight-backed, supple body. Her face was a dark oval, and although her features were indistinguishable, he had a feeling that she had not changed. Or perhaps it was that he hoped she had not changed.

He waited until some of the panic left him. Then he said: "You don't know how near I came to throwing lead at you."

"I knew I was taking that chance, Dane, but I had to see you, and I couldn't talk to you in the lobby. I don't want Ed to know I'm here."

He shut the door. "This fellow Ashton knows."

"I was in the livery stable when he came in. I saw him and jumped into a stall, but I wasn't sure whether he knew me or not."

Dane drew a match from his pocket and walked toward the bureau. "I'll light a lamp,"

"No, Dane. No light."

He stopped, his thumb pressed against the match head. "Why?"

"I know Ashton. It's my guess he's across the street, waiting for you to light a lamp. He's the kind who'd shoot you through the window."

"I figured that was his size." Dane put the match back into his pocket and moved toward her. "Sam must be getting old and jumpy to take on a hairpin like this Ashton."

"He's jumpy, all right," she said tonelessly. "He thinks the railroad and his town will make him a lot of money. Then he wants to go into politics. He's ... he's crazy, Dane. That's why I'm here."

He was close to her now, peering at her face in the darkness. He remembered her as a small and vital girl, filled with a great eagerness for living. Her hair had been the color of wheat straw, her eyes had been a dark blue, almost purple, but it was her mouth that he remembered better than any of her other features. At sixteen it had been full-lipped and sweetly shaped.

Now, reaching back into his memory, he thought of the last dance he had taken her to, of their kiss when he had brought her home, and his telling her he loved her. He'd told her he'd ask Drew for permission to marry her, and he remembered she'd grown tense in his arms as she'd said: "He won't let us, Dane. I know him too well."

She had been right. Now he wanted to reach out and take her

into his arms, to tell her that he had never stopped loving her and he still wanted to marry her no matter what sort of trouble there was between Sam Drew and his folks. But he didn't. He was not as impetuous as he had been four years before, and he knew what it would do to him if she drew away. She'd likely tell him that if he'd really loved her, he'd have written to her. He had no excuse. It was just that after he'd left the country, he had sworn to himself that he'd come back with a fortune in his pocket and he'd show Sam Drew that he was somebody. $52! What a hell of a fortune that was.

They stood peering into the darkness at each other, her face tilted up, but neither made any effort to touch the other. Four years was too long, too big a gap. His feelings had not changed, but hers probably had. Sixteen and twenty-one! A lot different than twenty and twenty-five. It was the difference between youth and maturity.

"You've come back a great man, Dane," she said at last. "We've heard a lot about you."

"Not a very great man," he said bitterly. "Not by Sam's standards."

"Sam's standards," she breathed. "You're still a fool, Dane. You're a fool because you can't see how small those standards are. Sometimes I think Rachel and I are the only ones who can."

Rachel was Drew's wife, a thin, frail woman who hated this country that Sam had brought her to. Dane had often thought when he'd seen her with Drew that she hated her husband as much as she hated the country.

"I reckon I'll find out how big he is," Dane said.

"I hope you will," she whispered. "I hope you will." She took a long breath. "Your dad has talked a lot about what you'll do when you get back. I guess he thinks you're ten feet tall and tougher than a boot heel."

"He's talked too much."

"He said one thing too much. He let it out when you'd be here. That's how Sam knew when to send Ed and Ashton. They aim to keep you out of the country or kill you."

"I know. Ed told me."

"What are you going to do?"

"I'll take the stage in the morning."

"No," she said sharply. "I don't want you to fight Ed, and that's what will happen if you stay here all night long."

"I ain't taking that train."

"I don't want you to. I've got horses in the alley. Mine and a bay I bought from the livery stable. He's not a very good horse, but it was the best I could do. We'll ride out."

"I ain't gonna pull you into trouble."

"None of that," she said angrily. "If you don't go, I'll stay right here and I'll be in the middle of it when Ed comes to put you on that train."

He was angry then. There would be trouble with Ed Lanning and Ashton when they came after him, and Becky wouldn't do anything but just be in the way. He said roughly: "No. You're leaving. I'm going to bed and getting some sleep."

"I'm not going." She put her hands on his arms and shook him. "Dane, you always were stubborn and I think you're worse now. You've got to go with me. You won't do any good by killing Ed and Ashton. It's up to you to make Sam do his own fighting."

There was some truth to what she said, but leaving now looked like running, and he'd never run from a fight in his life. "I'll do that job when the sign's right," he said doggedly.

She shook him again, her face white. "Dane, if you don't take me, what do you think Ashton will do to me? If he takes me back to Sam, I'll be in trouble. So will Rachel. She lied to Sam so I could come here."

He knew then that he had to go with her. Still he hesitated, fighting his own pride as he considered what Ashton would say when he got back to Prairie City. Dane Coe had backed out of a fight. He didn't have his tin star to hide behind, so he'd lit a shuck out of Ogallala. Well, he'd have to choke those words down

Ashton's throat, but now he had no choice.

"All right," he said. "I'll go."

She swung toward the window. "I think Ashton is over there to the left of the saloon. It's too dark to see for sure, but someone has been standing there a long time. That's why I didn't want you to light a lamp."

It took a moment for Dane to make out the figure on the boardwalk between the saloon and the building next to it. Then he saw him, a vague shadow that was a small man or a boy. Dane said: "It's probably him all right. Sam must want me out of the way mighty bad."

"He does. He's heard what you've done in Montana, and he's afraid of you." She turned toward the door. "I don't know where Ed is. He might be in the hall."

Dane picked up his war bag and saddle as Becky opened the door and looked down the dimly lit hall. She said: "No one here. We'll take the back stairs."

He followed her, not liking it. He didn't have a free hand for his gun. If either Ed Lanning or Ashton showed up, he'd be in a tight, but he reached the back stairs and went down them without trouble.

"Here," Becky breathed. "This is your horse."

There was some light in the alley from the back of the hotel. It took only a moment for Dane to saddle the bay and lash his war bag into place, then he stepped up and reined around.

"We'll circle Main Street ..." Becky began.

A shot stopped her words, the bullet snapping past close to Dane's head, the wink of powder flame showing at the other end of the alley. Digging in his spurs, Dane pulled his .44 and threw a shot at the gun flash. The other man fired again, wildly this time, for Dane and Becky were almost on him. Dane shot a second time, tilting his gun downward at the man. He heard a scream as the fellow dived sideways to get away from the driving hoofs, then they were out of the alley and heading south.

A racket rose behind them, some wild shooting and shouts, but no one barred their way. Presently they galloped across the South Platte, hoofs hammering on the plank flooring of the bridge, and then they were across it and the town was behind.

Dane reined up to listen, Becky stopping fifty feet beyond him. There was no sound of pursuit. They went on, riding up the long slope that led away from the river, and the prairie was all around them.

They rode steadily south, neither speaking, the empty land stretching away endlessly in all directions from them to cup upward to meet the down-sloping sky. From somewhere off to the west a coyote gave out his weird, nerve-tingling call, then there was the silence again, the silence and the eternal wind and the pressure of the black sky overhead that seemed to flatten out the earth.

Four years! A long time, the longest four years Dane Coe had ever known. Nights were not like this in Virginia City or Helena or Butte. He had almost forgotten how it was on the prairie, and he thought with some regret that it would be entirely different after the settlers came with their milk cows and wagons and plows to rip up the buffalo grass and plant grain, to wage their daily fight against the elements.

"Dane."

It was the first word she had spoken in an hour. He turned to her, a vague, slim shape in the blackness. He said: "What is it?"

"Why didn't you write, Dane?"

It was a question she had been bound to ask, but he had not wanted to hear it because there was no answer. He said: "I don't know. I guess I just figured you wouldn't want to wait for me."

"You must have met a lot of girls up there."

"None that I liked." He paused, wondering what she wanted him to say and thinking of the $52 in his pocket. "I guess that mostly I've been hoping I'd get lucky and make a fortune. Then I could come back and shove it under Sam's nose, and he'd have to let me marry you."

"Didn't you ever think it was me you wanted to marry, not Sam Drew?"

"Sure, but no one bucks Sam in his own home, not you or Rachel or anyone else. Not even Ed Lanning. Why Ed keeps on working for Sam I don't know."

She was silent for a time as if thinking about that. Finally she said: "That's been the trouble, Dane. Somebody has to buck Sam. No one likes him and a lot of people hate him, but we're all afraid of him. Even Rachel. That's hell, as near to hell as a person can get on this earth. I mean to have to live with a man you hate and fear like she does Sam."

Again the silence ran on. He wanted to tell her how he felt, that he had never stopped loving her, but it wasn't possible to ignore these years that made a gap between them. She would probably say he'd had a fine way of showing it, running off and not even sending her a card. What did he expect her to do, wait for him until she was an old maid? No, he couldn't tell her now.

The miles fell behind. They swung down into a long draw and came up on the other side again, the horses' hoofs dropping into the soft dust and stirring it around them. Presently a light showed ahead, and Becky said: "That's Prothro's roadhouse. We'd better spend the night there. I'm awfully tired."

"All right," he said.

He remembered Prothro's, a low, sod house that served as a stage stop, and he remembered old Prothro whose tongue dripped with all the gossip that came his way. They reached it and Becky called: "Prothro!" The house itself was dark. The light they had seen was a lantern that Prothro had hung in front of his door.

Becky called again: "Prothro!" A moment later the door swung open on its leather hinges, and the man came out, rubbing his eyes, white hair disheveled. He had slipped his pants on over his nightgown, and now he stood yawning as if sleep refused to relax its grip upon him.

"Prothro, this is my husband, Dane Coe," Becky said calmly.

Dane looked at her sharply, not thinking he had heard right. He opened his mouth to say something, and then shut it without saying anything. There was nothing a man could say under these circumstances.

Old Prothro had come suddenly awake. He said: "The hell! Sam'll kill him, Becky. Does your man know that?"

Becky slid down, ignoring Prothro's question, and stretched. She moved toward the house, saying: "Come on, Dane. Prothro will put the horses away."

"I don't like this," Prothro said. "Sam'll skin me and hang my hide out to dry for putting you up."

"We're staying here," Becky said. "It's too far to go home, and I'm tired."

"You'd be loco to go home. If you was smart, you'd be high-tailing the other way."

Dane stepped down, puzzled. It struck him then that Becky was playing her own game. He followed her into the house, Prothro standing there, staring after him.

"He's got just the one room," Becky said. "It's empty or he'd have said something."

She lit a lamp and carried it to the door at the east end of the house. Dane stood rooted at the table, staring after her, his mind gripping this and still finding no explanation. Becky opened, the door and went in. When he didn't come, she called sharply: "Come on, Dane! Don't stand there like you're paralyzed." She paused, and then added: "You're one man who can't be afraid of Sam. Not if the things they say about you are true."

He went then, Becky shutting the door behind him. He asked: "What's this all about?"

She said nothing for a moment, just stood there with her eyes on him as if uncertain what he would do or say. It was the first look he'd had of her in the light. The things he remembered were just as they had been—the wheat-yellow hair, the blue eyes that were almost purple, the sweet, full-lipped mouth.

There was one change he had not been aware of before, the maturity that four years had brought to her body, the roundness of breasts and the full curves of hips and thighs. And there was something else that was less tangible, a sort of inward confidence and determination that she had lacked as a girl.

Suddenly she turned and sat down on the bed. "Dane, I saved your life tonight. Now I'm asking something from you."

"What's that?"

She took a long breath. "There are a lot of things I ought to tell you but I can't make myself do it. Just trust me, will you, Dane? I want Sam to think we're married." She held up her left hand to show him the wedding ring she was wearing. "I even bought this to make it sound good."

He sensed that she had not done this because she loved him or because she really wanted to marry him. She was playing her own game, and Dane was remembering that Ed Lanning had said Drew had plans for her.

"What do you want me to do?" he asked.

"I want to rest here till sunup." She motioned to a chair. "You can sit there, and I'll lie here. When it's daylight, we'll ride. I ... I may go home with you for a while."

"And if Sam shows up, you'll tell him we're married?"

She looked at him defiantly. "That's right."

"And if Sam asks me, you want me to say it's true?"

"Is that too much for you to do?" she demanded.

"No, but you wanted him cut down to size. Just how do you figure I'll do it?"

"I don't know about things like that. You do, if half the stories we've heard about you are true. I'm fighting for myself, Dane, and for Rachel. She's the only friend I've got."

"You've got me."

"I hope so," she said hesitantly as if not quite sure. "Maybe I've got Ed Lanning, but sometimes I think that fighting Sam is like trying to stop a river with my hand. He always has his own way sooner or later."

She lay back on the bed. A moment later he heard her even breathing and thought she was asleep. He sat down in the one chair in the room, and only then did he realize how bone-tired he was. He stretched his legs out in front of him, his chin dipping down to his chest, and fell asleep.

III

It seemed only a moment before Dane was awake again. Daylight was driving the shadows from the room. He was aware of two things at once. Becky was gone and, outside, Ed Lanning was shouting: "Open up, Prothro! Open up or we'll smash your door down!"

Dane came to his feet and checked his gun. He had no idea where Becky had gone, but he did know he had trouble on his hands. Probably Frank Ashton was with Lanning. He stepped out into the big living room. Prothro had opened the front door, and Dane heard him say: "I tell you that's all I know. They rode in about midnight. Becky said Coe was her husband. I put the horses away, and they went to bed."

"Get 'em up," Lanning said angrily.

Dane crossed the room and pushed Prothro aside. Lanning was standing in front of the door, his bony face dark as thunder. Ashton was behind him, his lips swollen and bruised. Dane said: "I'm up."

"Where's Becky?"

"I don't know. She ain't in the room."

"Get out of the way," Lanning said. "I'm going to look."

Dane stepped out into the pale morning light and put his back against the sod wall of the house. Lanning went inside. Dane pinned his gaze on Ashton. Desire was bright in the man's pale eyes. Dane understood how it was with him. Life was a simple thing to men like Frank Ashton; they were never faced by difficult decisions. A gun could settle anything. Too, Ashton was driven by an inordinate pride. Yesterday he had been humiliated by Dane Coe. Today he would wipe that humiliation out with his gun.

Behind him Dane heard Lanning shout: "Where'd she go, Prothro?" And Prothro answered: "How the hell would I know? I told her Sam would kill Coe for this. Maybe she got scared and ran."

"Her horse in the stable?"

"Dunno. Didn't look."

"Then look, damn it!"

There was this moment of talk, Prothro and Lanning behind Dane, Ashton crouching in front. The gunman was going to draw. Dane knew that from the look on his narrow, red-splotched face, the fire glowing in his pale eyes. His bruised lips were pulled away from his gums, showing the hole where the tooth had been that Dane had knocked out the day before.

As Lanning and Prothro tramped across the front room, Ashton's right hand moved toward his gun. Then Lanning was in the door, shouting—"Hold it, Frank!"—but he was too late. Ashton's hand was already sweeping downward.

There was no choice for Dane Coe. This moment had been destined from the instant he had knocked Ashton down in Ogallala's Main Street. He made his draw, the same swift draw that had given him his reputation in the Montana mining camps. Both guns thundered, blasting apart the morning silence. Powder flame pierced the long shadow thrown by the sod house.

There was no time between the shots, for they came as one sound. Ashton's bullet drove into the sod wall behind Dane, missing his head by an inch. Dane's bullet took Ashton in the chest and knocked him flat into the hoof-trodden earth in front of the road-house. He lay there, motionless, one hand thrown out, the other under him, his gun a foot from his body.

Dane wheeled to Lanning. "You buying into this, Ed?"

"No," Lanning said. "Not today. Go see about Becky's horse, Prothro."

Prothro walked toward his stable, a bent, worried old man. Lanning stood facing Dane, his lips squeezed tightly against his teeth, all the good humor gone out of him.

Dane said: "Tie your man on his horse, Ed, and start riding."

Lanning didn't move. He said: "I don't give a damn about Ashton, but I'll kill you for what you've done to Becky."

"You've got this wrong, Ed," Dane said quietly.

"The hell I have! I tried to get you not to come down here, but you wouldn't listen. I figured Sam was wrong about you, but he wasn't. He said you'd play hell, and you sure have." Lanning took a long breath, his nostrils quivering. "You asked me yesterday why I kept working for Sam. I'll tell you. I love Becky. If I quit, I'd never see her again. She won't have me, but she needs a friend. That's why I'll kill you before I'm done."

"You've got this wrong, Ed," Dane said again. "Becky needs us both."

Lanning swung away and strode toward Ashton's body. He lifted it into saddle and tied it there. Then Prothro called from the stable: "Becky's horse is gone, Lanning."

Without another word Lanning stepped up and rode south, leading Ashton's horse. He did not look back. Dane swung toward the stable. Prothro said: "You owe me a dollar for the bed."

Dane tossed him a silver dollar and went past him into the low-roofed sod stable. He saddled the bay and mounted. Prothro still stood there, his lined face troubled. He said: "It ain't no skin off my nose, but, was I you, I'd get to hell out of this country or you'll get what your brother Fred did."

Dane looked down at the old man, suddenly sick with fear. He should have guessed that something had happened to Fred. Becky had wanted to tell him something, but she had been unable to make herself say it. Dane asked hoarsely: "What happened to Fred?"

"He was shot in the back three days ago when he was riding home from Prairie City."

"Who did it?"

"I don't know. Ashton, maybe."

Dane nodded and rode away. He had come back too late.

IV

Meadowlarks made the morning sweet all around Dane. Blackbirds took wing in front of his horse and lit on swaying grass stems, taking up their songs again. The wind came quartering in from the southwest, hot and dry, and all around Dane the buffalo grass made a crinkly, soft-green carpet that stretched away for endless miles of gently rolling prairie.

These were the things that Dane ordinarily would have seen and heard and felt. They were things that he had missed these four years. Today he was aware of none of them. He rode with his head tipped down, his thoughts on his brother, and he was remembering Fred's words the day he had left the Frenchman: "You're running out, Dane. We need you, and we'll always need you."

Still, there was no regret in Dane. He'd done what, at the time, he'd had to do. They hadn't needed him on the BC. He'd sent money back. It wasn't as if he had cut his family ties. But Fred did not deserve to die. He had been a mild, gentle boy, and he had not changed as a man.

Dane remembered how Fred had fallen into the habit of repeating many of their father's platitudes. Everything was always all right, the world was a good place, and in the end the wrong would be punished and the right would win. The truth of the matter was that neither Fred nor Bill Coe was tough enough to survive in this lawless country. Perhaps that was why they sought strength in the repetition of empty words.

To Dane there had never been anything very realistic in Fred's and his father's philosophy, and he had sensed that they were distrustful of his. Still, Fred had said they needed him. He understood, although at the time it hadn't made much sense. It was just that he had been the fighter in the family, the hard-headed, skeptical one who took after his mother, and Fred and his father had leaned upon him.

Near noon Dane stopped at a spring and watered his horse and took a drink. He went on, his thoughts coming now to Becky. He could think of a dozen explanations of her leaving during the night, but none seemed to fit. She had probably gone home to whatever trouble faced her. Dane knew what his own course would be. He had to see her, no matter what Sam Drew would think or do.

It was midafternoon when Dane reached the BC. There were no changes in its appearance—the same squat sod house and sheds and barn, the wire corrals, the tall windmill whirling and clattering, the field of wheat beyond the house.

Bill Coe had always said that sooner or later the farmers would come as they so often came to the cattle country. There was no use to fight them as most cowmen did; it would be like trying to hold back the tide. Bill Coe would never be a farmer, but he liked to experiment with different grains. When the settlers did come, there were things he would be able to tell them. They would ask him for his advice and they would respect him.

They saw Dane before he reached the house, and they stood in front of the door, waiting for him. They had aged more than four years should have aged them. Bill Coe's beard was completely white. His mother's hair that had been dark brown was gray, and time had chiseled lines in their faces that had not been there when he'd left.

No one felt like talking for a time. He put his arms around his mother and kissed her and held her hard against him. He took his father's hand and saw the tears in his eyes. Bill Coe had never been one to hide his emotions. Dane went into the house with them, and he stood looking around, feeling the heat from the range, smelling the new bread that his mother had just taken from the oven, seeing the pictures on the plastered walls that had been hanging there as long as they had lived on the Frenchman.

Bill Coe cleared his throat. "You're looking well, Dane."

"And a little thin," his mother said. She looked at the gun on his hip and brought her eyes back to his face. "You're hungry?"

He nodded. "It's been a long time since I ate anything."

"I'll put your horse away," his father said, and left the room.

V

Mary Coe filled the firebox with buffalo chips and shoved the coffee pot to the front. She sliced ham into a frying pan, and put it on the stove. Then she turned to face him. "You know about Fred?"

"I heard this morning."

"We buried him yesterday." She swung back to the stove. "We don't know who did it. Frank Ashton probably."

"Why?"

She peeled a potato and sliced it into the frying pan. "It's Sam Drew, of course, but there's no proof."

"Fred never hurt anyone," Dane said.

"Drew wants us to sell out. That's the answer to everything. If you ride east about a mile, you'll see the railroad grade. The company plans to build this far. Paw has already staked out a town site. He's talked to the company, and they favor it for the end of steel, but Drew wants to stop the railroad in Prairie City. If he can't do that, he wants to own the town that will be the end of track. I guess he thought that with you gone and Fred dead, we'd give up."

Dane took a drink of water from the dipper that hung above the bucket just inside the door, thinking of what Drew had done to keep him from coming back. A moment later his father came in.

"That ain't a real good horse you're riding," Bill Coe said.

"I got him in Ogallala."

"I suspicioned that. Well, you remember old Nancy's colt, Blackie? He's a right good horse, Dane. You take him."

"Thanks. I'll need a fresh horse."

"Where are you going?" his mother asked.

Dane's gaze turned to his mother.

"I told you, Paw," she said. "Being Dane, it's the only thing he can do. Becky's still home, Dane, and she ain't never married."

His mother set the meal on the table, and sliced the fresh bread. While he ate, Dane told them what had happened at Ogallala and at Prothro's. They listened in silence, his mother's face inscrutable, his father's tense with emotion.

When Dane had finished, Bill Coe shook his head. "Nothing can fetch Fred back. Drew had been threatening us. Then one night a bunch of 'em rode in and fired some shots. The next day Fred said he was going to stop Drew. He said that was what you'd do if you was here. I don't know what happened in town. He didn't get back by noon like he said he would, so we started looking. We found him about two miles east of here."

Dane got up and walked to the door. The Frenchman lay just to the south, a spring-fed stream that took a lazy course to the southeast. Beyond it were the sand hills, low ridges that lifted toward the horizon. He thought absently that the farmers might make out here on the hard ground, but the sand hills would always be cattle range.

"Maybe you shouldn't go," Bill Coe urged. "I've done a lot of bragging about you. They'll be set the minute you ride in."

Dane glanced up at the sun. It was low in the west. He heard his mother say: "Don't try to change him, Paw. He's got to make up his own mind."

"It'll be evening by the time I get there." Dane turned to look at his mother's sun-blackened face. The garden beyond the windmill was hers, and through the first years they had lived here that garden had been half of their living. "I'll be back by midnight, I reckon."

His mother nodded, holding her lips tightly against the feeling that was in her. She said: "You're all we have now, Dane."

She allowed herself to say that. No more.

Dane said: "I'll be back. Been a long time since I've slept in my own bed."

"A long time," she said, and stood in the doorway while he walked with his father to the barn.

Dane stepped in beside the mare Nancy and patted her neck, talking to her. Then he lifted his saddle to the black gelding in the next stall, and tightened the cinches. "He's a good horse," Dane said. "Ain't built much like Nancy."

"Fastest animal in the country," Bill Coe said with pride.

Dane stepped into the saddle and sat for a moment, looking down at his father. He said: "Don't worry none."

Bill said, tight-lipped: "I ain't never been a brave man. I've been long on talk and full of big ideas. I know they call me Windy Bill Coe, but if I live, I'll show 'em I ain't just talk. We'll have the county seat right here, and we'll see this country filled with settlers just like I've always said, but that ain't neither here nor there. You'll need a hand when you get to Prairie City. I'll go along."

"No, I'll make out better by myself." Dane scratched the back of his neck, feeling for the right words. He said slowly: "I don't claim to be a brave man, neither, Paw. I've been afraid plenty of times, and I'll be afraid when I get to Prairie City, but it'll work out."

"Sure," Bill Coe said. "It'll work out."

Dane smiled as he rode away, leading the bay he had ridden from Ogallala. He lifted a hand to his mother, then he rode east, and he was thinking: *That's just what Fred would have said. It'll work out.*

A mile east of the BC buildings Dane came to the railroad grade. He followed it to Prairie City.

Apparently no work had been done on it for several days, and that struck Dane as being strange. If the company had not intended to build as far as Bill Coe's town, it would have stopped the grading at Prairie City. On the other hand, if the plan was to go on, why had the work been stopped? The answer to that, Dane thought, lay ahead of him in Sam Drew's town.

Within the hour Dane came to the first homestead, part dugout and part soddy, with a nondescript-looking milk cow standing on the roof, placidly chewing her cud. A skinny boy in patched overalls and battered straw hat came through the door and waved at Dane, then climbed the bank after the cow. Dane rode on, stirred by the scene, for it meant a great deal. This had been S Star range as long as the Coes lived here, and it seemed strange that a man like Sam Drew would make no effort to hold the settlers back.

The sun was almost down when Dane rode into Prairie City, his shadow long in front of him. The town itself was exactly as he remembered it. A general store, a saloon, a hotel, and a livery stable occupied frame buildings on the corners made by the intersection of a side street. Half a dozen sod houses were scattered haphazardly around, and to the south of main street the raw earth of the railroad grade made a fresh wound on the face of the prairie. That was the only change four years had brought to Prairie City.

It was suppertime, and that, Dane thought, was probably the reason no one was on the street. He swung left to the S Star buildings, fifty yards or more north of the town. Drew had built Prairie City as a trading center for the few ranchers that were scattered along the Frenchman and the transients who drifted through the country, but more specifically Drew had put up the saloon for his own cowhands.

It was common talk that by the end of the month the wages Drew paid his men had trickled back into his own pockets. Now the railroad meant an end to what had been a cattle empire. Drew would have to sell his herd or move. Either way, he meant for his town to more than make up the loss to him.

Dane reined up in front of the S Star ranch house, a two-story frame building that had been painted a violent red as long as Dane could remember. Both Rachel and Becky objected to the color, but Drew refused to change it. It was distinctive, he said. Anyone who passed by would see it and remember it, and they'd remember Sam Drew.

There was no activity around the ranch as Dane dismounted and tied his gelding and the bay. That in itself was an ominous sign, which Dane noted. He paused for a moment, eyes swinging to the bunkhouse, and on to the barns and sheds. A few horses were in corrals. There was no other sign of life.

Dane swung around the hitch rack and crossed the barren yard to the porch. The front door was open, and he could hear the murmur of woman talk from the back of the house. He knocked, and presently heard steps cross the living room. Rachel Drew appeared in the doorway. She looked at him for a moment, then recognition flowed across her pale face, and she stepped back as if frightened.

"Dane." She whispered his name, a skinny hand coming up to her throat. "Go away, Dane. You can't come here."

"I brought Becky's horse back," he said. "I want to see her."

"You can't. They'll kill you." She seemed to sense that she was saying the wrong thing. "Becky doesn't want to see you. She's going through with it."

"Through with what?"'

"Didn't she tell you?"

"She didn't tell me much of anything. She didn't even say that Fred had been dry-gulched."

"Go away, Dane. Go away. Nobody can help us. It'll just mean trouble, and there's been enough."

VI

Dane stood there, looking at Sam Drew's wife. She was thirty-five, years younger than Drew, but she looked older, much older than she had the last time he'd seen her. He remembered when he had first seen her. He had been a boy, and Becky had been a girl with taffy-colored pigtails down her back, but at that time Dane had looked at Rachel, not Becky. Rachel had been pretty then with color in her cheeks. She'd had some pride and some courage, but now it seemed that both were gone.

"I'm going to see Becky. Don't try to stop me," Dane said. "Is she here?"

She gestured wearily. "Come in. She's here."

Dane followed her through the big living room and along a hall into a small room in the back of the house. Becky was sitting at a sewing machine, working on some white, flimsy material, the lamp beside her throwing a yellow glow upon her hair. She turned her head and her lips came open at the shock of seeing Dane.

"Dane! Are you crazy coming here?"

"Daft as a loon." He moved into the room, putting his feet down carefully to avoid stepping on pieces of dress pattern and odds and ends of cloth that were scattered on the floor. "Did you think I wouldn't?"

"Of course I didn't think you'd come. I thought you'd be mad at me." She rose, her gaze moving to Rachel who stood in the doorway. "Why did you let him in?"

"He's stubborn," Rachel said. "Almost as stubborn as Sam."

"Don't say that," Becky protested. "He's not like Sam, not in any way."

She turned her head, her hands clenched on the sewing machine, and she began to cry. Dane had never seen her cry before. Somehow she had always seemed above the usual feminine weaknesses. It struck Dane now that if she kept on living this way, she would be like Rachel in a few years. She had lost the confidence and determination he had seen in her at Prothro's. Her coming back to the S Star had done that. Sam Drew had a way of destroying anything he touched.

"She's working on her wedding dress," Rachel said tonelessly. "You'd better tell him, Becky."

"Wedding dress?" Dane asked incredulously. "Who are you gonna marry?"

Becky faced him, blinking the tears out of her eyes. "I'm sorry, Dane. I didn't want you to see me cry. I'm supposed to marry Jim Wardell."

"Who's Wardell?"

"A railroad man. He's the one who'll make the decision about how far they lay steel. He's been after me to marry him from the time he first came here, but I hate him, Dane. I couldn't stand it."

"No," Rachel said. "You couldn't."

"Sam can't make you marry anybody," Dane said. "He can do a lot of things, but he can't do that."

"I guess you don't know Sam very well." Becky sat down, her hands folded on her lap. "He's never told me I had to. If you ask him, he'd say he wasn't making me do anything. He works on everyone who is my friend. Like Rachel and Ed Lanning. And you. That's why I went to Ogallala, Dane. I thought I could scheme better than he could, but it's no use."

"You told Prothro that we were married because you knew Prothro would spread it," Dane said, "and you thought that when Sam heard, he'd let up. That it?"

"That's it," she answered honestly, "but I couldn't get out of my mind what Prothro had said about Sam killing you, and if I went to your home, he'd send his men there. I'd just bring trouble to your people, and they've had enough."

"So you ran."

He said it with cool contempt, and it angered her. "Don't talk to me that way. I've spent most of the four years since you left hating you. When Sam said you couldn't marry me, you were the one who ran. You were afraid of him just like we all are."

He lowered his eyes, knowing that she had a right to hate him, but she was wrong about his being afraid of Sam Drew. It was his pride that had sent him away. Now it seemed that his intention to make a fortune and shove it under Sam Drew's nose had been a little foolish. It would take more than money to change Drew. Sam was using Becky for his own profit just as he would have used an animal he owned, or someone like Frank Ashton who could be hired.

"I'll find Sam," Dane said.

He started to turn, but Becky came to her feet, crying: "No, Dane! There's nothing you can do. You can feel things so long, and then you're done. You get numb and sort of hollow inside. You just ... just live to work and eat and sleep. That's the way I feel now. I can't go on holding out against him."

Dane reached for her and put his arm around her. "Listen, Becky. Right now you think you're past feeling, but you aren't. If you marry this Jim Wardell, you'll find out how it is. You'll hate him and you'll hate yourself and maybe you'll kill him."

"That's what I've told her," Rachel said "but it's no use. She thinks that by marrying Wardell she'll save you."

"Rachel. You promised ..."

"I know," Rachel said, "and I'm breaking that promise. Maybe

Dane will get killed before morning. Maybe he won't. And if he doesn't, we'll all be happier."

They heard heavy steps cross the living room and come along the hall. Rachel stepped into the room and stood beside Becky. Dane put a hand on his gun and held it there until Sam Drew stood in the doorway, his big body almost filling it, great head tilted forward so that his fat double chin flowed out across his chest. There was a sense of power about Drew. It was there in his thick body, his pillar of a neck, his dark brown eyes that had a way of boring into a man. He was like a block of granite set in the channel of a rushing river, set so solidly it could not be moved.

"It's been four years, Sam," Dane said. "I'm back."

"And you won't be here long. I thought I'd find you here when I saw the horses." He jerked his head toward the hall. "You've brought disgrace to us. Prothro will tell everybody who goes by that you and Becky spent the night at his place."

"Show him your wedding ring, Becky," Dane said, keeping his eyes on Drew's face.

"You don't need to bother," Drew said. "Don't make me no never mind, either way. Wardell still wants her. If you did marry her, we can make a widow out of her mighty damned quick."

"Why don't you do that, Sam?" Dane said softly. "Now."

"Not before my women." Drew smiled a little.

"I didn't get all the story," Dane said, "but I got the notion that this Wardell has promised to stop the railroad here if Becky married him. That right?"

"It's about the size of it," Drew admitted. "It's a good deal for all of us. I get the end of steel and the county seat. Becky gets a man who can give her a good home."

"And you go unhung for killing Fred." Dane shook his head. "I'm going to kill you, Sam. I don't believe in a man taking justice into his own hands, but this time it's the only thing that can be done."

The smile was set now on Drew's face. "I don't think you will,

bucko. I'll tell you why. You'll die when you step out of this house."
Drew turned and tramped back down the hall.

Becky gripped Dane's arm. "You see? If you'd stayed away, everything would have been all right. Now I can't save you."

"Funny how Sam's got a way of making folks believe that what he says will happen." Dane looked down at her, thinking how much depended on this next hour. "I learned one thing packing a star. The trouble in the world comes from just a few people. As long as they're free to kick things around, you're going to keep on having trouble."

"But here you're just one man," Rachel said somberly, "and you don't have a star."

Dane was only half listening. He was still looking down at Becky, and he was seeing in her face something he had not been sure of before. "Becky, when you went to Ogallala, you thought you hated me because I left without seeing you and I never wrote, so you thought you could use me to save yourself. That true?"

She nodded. "That's right."

"Then after we were together you found out you didn't hate me at all. Maybe you found out you did care about what happened to me. That's why you left, ain't it?"

She nodded again. "But it doesn't really change anything."

"Why, it changes everything. Now I'm ten feet tall and tougher'n a boot heel." He swung to Rachel. "Where will I find this Wardell?"

"Probably in his hotel room. It's Number Twelve."

He stepped past Rachel and went out of the room and into the kitchen, ignoring Becky's: "Dane ... Dane, don't go!" At that moment he actually felt ten feet tall and tougher than a boot heel.

Sam Drew was both confident and careful. As far as Dane knew, the man had never made a mistake in handling a situation like this. Or if he had, he had kept it a secret. It explained the legend of success that had grown up around him. It was the reason Becky had said that everyone was afraid of him. No one wanted to fight a man who could not be whipped.

VII

Dane moved slowly across the big kitchen, feeling his way until he came to the table in the middle of the room. He had shut the door so that no light came from the sewing room, but he remembered that the back door opened onto a porch. Drew would have men waiting out there for him, and he'd have some more waiting in front, and they'd open up on him the minute he came out of the house.

There were three windows in the long east wall of the kitchen. Dane paused, feeling the heat that was imprisoned here in the room. It was a black night, black enough to give him a chance to get clear if he made a run across the porch, but it was not a good chance, for he would have to lunge through a patch of lamplight coming from the windows of the sewing room. Drew's men would be watching that patch of lamplight.

It was no time for haste. Dane stood there a long time, thinking of this. His job was to get to Sam Drew. He doubted that anyone had ever faced Drew and bullied him into a fight. The reason was partly the appearance of unconquerable strength that Drew was able to project, and partly his talent for having someone else to do his fighting for him.

It was Dane's guess that Drew had watched him ride into town and enter the house. Then he had come in, knowing that Dane would not pull his gun in the presence of Becky and Rachel unless forced to, and Drew had been careful to avoid that. Drew may have gone back to where he had been, probably the saloon, or he might be outside, satisfied to let the night hide him. Wardell was the weakness in Drew's position. Dane's problem was to get to Wardell.

Carefully Dane went over the possibilities in his mind. He could go back and ask Becky to blow out the lamp in the sewing room, but to do that would focus attention on the back porch. He could go out through the front door, but that was exactly what Drew would expect, and it was likely where he had placed most of his men. The windows were the other choice.

Dane moved toward them, hoping he would find one open. He could not raise one without bringing them down upon him, for he was bound to make a racket. He moved along the wall. The first window was closed. So was the second, but the third was open and there was no screen. Dane stood there a moment, peering into the darkness and feeling the cool night air. He could not see anyone, and he heard nothing that would indicate a man was out here on this side of the house.

Slowly Dane slipped out through the window, easing down to the ground and crouching there, right hand on his gun. There had been a faint whisper of sound as he'd slid over the sill, but he had no idea how far it would carry or how close Drew's men would be. He had no doubt that someone was here, for it was inconceivable that Drew would leave the side of the house unguarded.

The minutes ticked away. Dane had a talent for waiting, and this sort of thing was not new to him. Waiting tightens a man's nerves until he must do something, move about or talk or fire a cigarette. Anything to break the tension. Sooner or later the guard would give away his position. When he did, there was a chance Dane could worm his way past him and circle to the back of the hotel.

VIII

The break came, but not in the way Dane had expected. A man came around the back corner of the house, calling softly: "Any sign of him, Ed?"

Lanning, not more than thirty feet from where Dane crouched, said: "Not a damned thing."

"What the hell's he doing in there?" the man asked irritably. "I'm getting tired of sitting around."

"He's probably with Becky," Lanning said in a dry, sullen tone. "He'll be out, come sunup."

"That's a long time to wait," the man said sourly. "I've got a notion to root him out."

"Go ahead," Lanning said. "Sam'll give you an extra five dollars. It'll help bury you."

"Aw, reckon I ain't in no hurry." The man moved back around the corner.

Dane waited a full minute. Then he drew his gun, whispering: "Don't shoot, Ed. I've got a question to ask you."

There was no answer. Dane was sure that Lanning was close enough to hear. He said: "Listen to me, Ed. Are you gonna have a hand in this deal with Wardell?"

Still no answer. Dane went on. "I told you she needed both of us. There's no one but you and me who think enough of her to get her out of this. Or maybe you don't love her enough to help. Maybe you were just lying."

"Damn you," Lanning breathed. "Damn you to hell. I love her enough to kill you for what you done to her at Prothro's."

"I didn't touch her, Ed. She aimed for Sam to hear we were married so Wardell would give her up. Then she got to thinking she'd get me in trouble, and she pulled out."

Lanning was silent then. Dane had no way of telling what was going on in the man's head. He moved toward Lanning, belly flat, gun held in front of him, then stopped within fifteen feet of the S Star ramrod. He said: "Ed, you know what Sam is better'n I do. You ain't the kind to keep on doing his dirty work. Look at him, Ed, raising Becky like she was his own girl and then using her to fill his pockets. Selling her like he would a thoroughbred filly, and you're helping."

Lanning was thinking about it, uncertain of himself, or he would have opened up with his gun. Dane moved forward again, faster now. In the thin starlight he could make out the man's high, angular body. Then Lanning said: "All right, Dane. What do you aim to do?"

"Find Wardell. All I want is a chance to get at Sam."

"Wardell's in his hotel room," Lanning said. "Come on."

Dane could not trust the foreman. He had seen the black, unforgiving hate in Lanning's face that morning at Prothro's. It was not likely he would completely change, but he had to take the chance that Lanning was not a man who would shoot him in cold blood. It was a chance he could not have taken with Ashton, but it was a good gamble with Lanning.

"That's better," Dane said, and coming to his feet, took two steps that brought him close to Lanning. He could not see the foreman's face in the darkness; it was a light splotch between his dark Stetson and shirt. Dane could not tell where his hands were and whether he was holding his gun.

"Stand there," Lanning ordered. "I'll see you get your chance at Sam."

Dane dived forward, his head driving into Lanning's hard stomach. The foreman grunted as breath went out of him. Dane swung his left, and he got Lanning high on the face. Off balance and winded, he went down, Dane on top of him. Dane swung his gun, catching him solidly-across the head. Lanning went limp under him.

IX

It was a question of time now. There had been no loud sound and their voices had been kept low, but the man behind the house might have heard. If he had, he'd have the pack after Dane within a matter of seconds.

Dane ran, swinging away from the house. A man called—"Ed?"—and Dane knew his luck had curdled on him. He angled toward the hotel, and someone at the house yelled: "Hey, Ed's out cold!" And then Drew's great voice: "Get him! Five hundred dollars to the man who burns him down!"

The rear of the hotel was dark, but Dane had not forgotten how it was. There was a back door in the middle and stairs that led to the long hall that bisected the second story. He found the door and jerked it open. Someone was firing wildly at the sound of his steps, then he pulled the door shut behind him, locked it, and ran up the stairs.

There was a wall bracket lamp about halfway down the hall, leaving both ends dimly lit. Room Twelve should be about where the lamp was. He passed Ten. Twelve was the next. He turned the knob. The door was locked. He drew back and slammed into it, smashing it open with his foot. He spilled into the room, almost falling as a man sitting beside a desk near the window turned his head.

Dane regained his balance and kicked the door shut. He asked:

"You Jim Wardell?"

The man rose, his face frozen with the fear that gripped him. He blinked behind the heavy lenses of his glasses. He looked at the gun and brought his gaze back to Dane's face. "I'm Wardell. What do you want?"

"I'm Dane Coe."

The man sat down again, quickly as if his knees could not hold his weight. He said hoarsely: "I thought they had you penned up in the house."

"The pen didn't hold me. Get up. You're coming with me."

"I don't have any part in your squabbles. Leave me alone."

"Wardell, the one thing I ain't got is time. Get up!"

Drew's men were smashing at the back door, then Drew bawled: "We'll go through the front! Barton, stay here! We'll keep him bottled up!"

Wardell seemed to lack the strength to bring himself to his feet. Dane grabbed him by the nape of his neck and yanked him to the door. He got him into the hall and to the head of the stairs when someone in the lobby yelled: "Look out! Old man Coe's here."

Dane went down the stairs in a headlong rush, leaving Wardell in the hall. It was inconceivable to Dane that his father was here, Bill Coe who admitted he had always been long on words and short on doing. But he was here, standing at the desk and facing the door, double-barreled shotgun in his hands. Directly in front of him, massed in the doorway, were Drew's men.

Dane yelled—"Hold it, Paw!"—and took the last three steps in one long jump to the lobby, but there was no holding Bill Coe. He pulled the shotgun to his shoulder and let go just as the men in the doorway sprawled into the lobby, crawling frantically to get out of the range of the buckshot. By falling aside that way, they had left Sam Drew unprotected. He went back, crying out in agony, stumbling in a wild effort to regain his balance, then he spilled backward off the boardwalk and fell into the dust.

X

There was a moment of silence while the echoes of the shotgun blast died. The S Star men who were inside the lobby got to their feet to face Dane, but there was no fight in them now. They looked into the muzzle of Dane's gun and slowly brought their hands above their heads. Then Ed Lanning stood in the doorway, and he looked across the lobby at Dane, saying: "Put your gun up, boy. Sam's dead, and there'll be nobody wasting any tears over him."

"You want to buy into this now?"

"No," Lanning said. "I just talked to Becky."

"Who killed Fred?" Dane asked.

Lanning motioned toward the street. "Sam. Drygulching is his way."

Bill Coe had dropped his shotgun. He looked at Dane, then wiped a hand across his face. "I thought I'd give you a hand, but I didn't think I'd ever kill a man."

"Let's say it was an execution," Dane said quietly. Turning, he pinned his eyes on Wardell who had come halfway down the stairs, a pale-faced, trembling man. "You had things all figured out, Wardell, but your scheme won't work."

"I didn't have any scheme." Wardell licked dry lips. "Drew promised us free land in his town for our depot and shops."

"You've got a grade built almost to Coeburg," Dane said. "Paw will give the railroad as much as Drew promised."

"Sure," Bill Coe said, "and more. What about it, Wardell?"

Wardell licked his lips again, struggling for strength to stay on his feet. Then he said in a low tone: "We'll lay steel on that grade, Mister Coe. Your town will be the end of track."

"I'll hold you to that promise," Dane said, "or I'll skin you and hang your hide on the wall." He turned to his father. "Wait here, Paw. I want to see Becky."

He reached the corner and stopped, for Becky was standing there, pulled back against the wall of the hotel. She reached out and touched him, asking: "You all right, Dane?"

For a moment he stood looking at her, her face turned up to him. He said: "Sure, I'm all right." He took her arm, and they walked along the side street toward the S Star house.

"The railroad's here," Dane said, "and the settlers will be flooding the country in another year. We'll have a county and we'll have law, and it won't be Sam's law."

"No," she said, "and I'm pretty sure of one thing. You'll be the first sheriff ... of our county."

Our county! It was good to think of it that way. He said: "We can't make up for four years, Becky, but there are a lot of years ahead." He put his arms around her, and she gave him her lips, and they were sweet under his.

BLACK MIKE

.

I

Sam Cassidy braced his legs and hung onto the edge of the seat as the stage topped Tremont Pass and roared down the steep west slope. He glanced at the driver, Buck McHale, and grinned. McHale was a good Jehu who considered the day wasted if he didn't give the paid customers a thrill. Today Sam was returning home after being graduated from the University of Wyoming, so McHale was putting out a little extra effort for him.

Here, on the higher slopes, timber gave the Bearpaw range a dark covering as far as Sam could see to the north and south, but farther down the trees were smaller and scattered and eventually disappeared entirely on the lower, grass-covered slopes. Somewhere below them was the county seat, the town of Cañon where Sam had grown up.

McHale glanced at him, then shouted above the clatter of the coach: "What are you fixing to do, now that you're ejicated? Go to work in your pa's bank?"

"No, I'm going to read law in Judge Murray's office," Sam said. "I couldn't stand being cooped up in a bank adding a string of figures. Pa seems to like it, but it would drive me loco."

They reached the end of the steep section of the grade and slowed down. McHale stared at the straight stretch of road ahead of them, squinting against the sun. He said sourly: "No offense, Sam, but what your pa likes about the banking is saying no when a man asks for a loan."

"I'm afraid you're right," Sam said.

"You could go to work for old Ben Faraday," McHale said. "Reading law ain't gonna earn you no money. Ben tells me he's gonna give up sheriffing when his term's out and take it easy on his ranch."

"Doesn't seem fitting to go back to riding for thirty a month and beans after getting all this book learning."

"No it don't," McHale agreed, "but maybe you belong on a horse instead of arguing in a law court. You've been a hell-raiser as long as I can remember. There's still some signs on Main Street where you've dotted an *i* or two with a Forty-Five slug. Which makes me wonder how you ever managed to stay in college long enough to graduate."

"Ma wanted me to graduate and I'd do 'most anything for her," Sam said.

"It's a good reason," McHale said. "I guess everybody in Cañon loves your ma unless it's that bastard, Monk Corley. He don't love nobody except hisself."

"Monk still taking big steps like always?" Sam asked.

McHale nodded. "Like always. Gives orders to the Cowmen's Association like he owns the outfit. He even gives orders to your pa."

"It would be hard on the bank if he pulled his money out," Sam said.

"I s'pose," McHale grunted. "Well, you could get the deputy's job again. You toted the star last summer and done a good job. Only thing is the man who goes to work for Ben Faraday is just asking for dirt to be throwed in his face."

"What's wrong? I didn't have any trouble last year."

"No, Cañon County was downright peaceable last summer, but hell's boiling now and no mistake."

They were in the scattered timber, the road almost level, with a sharp drop-off to the right. McHale pointed ahead to two men who stood in the road, both holding revolvers in their hands, the small one motioning for the stage to stop.

"There's what's wrong," McHale said bitterly.

"Road agents?" Sam asked, staring at the two men and seeing that both were strangers.

"Nope," McHale said. "They're Monk Corley's hardcases. They've stopped me here for a week or more. All they want is to look over the passengers."

"Why?"

"It's a long story," McHale answered, "but mostly it's a case of Monk being afraid the sheepmen are sending in some gunslingers. He don't aim to let that happen."

"Oh, cut it out," Sam said. "Black Mike Nickels is the only sheepman in the county and he wouldn't bring in any gunmen."

"Yep, he's the only one unless you count his boys, Shawn and Rory," McHale said, "and young Pete who's herding the big band on Dutchman Flat."

They had reached the men in the road and McHale pulled the horses down and set the brake. He said: "I've got just one passenger. He's Jonas Cassidy's son Sam who's coming home from college, so get out of the road and let the stage by. I'm getting damned tired of you stopping me every day."

"So you're getting tired, are you, old man?" the small one said. "Well, sir, I'll tell you something. You're gonna get tireder of it than you are now."

"Get down," the big man ordered, nodding at Sam.

"Better do what he says," McHale said in a low tone, and added as if talking to himself: "Old man, am I? Someday I'll show that ornery booger how old I am."

Sam swung down and moved forward until he faced the two men in front of the stage. They were tough hands, the kind of barren-faced plug-uglies who thrived on trouble. In the past men like these two seldom came to Cañon. It was off the beaten path, a small town in a thinly populated county, and there had been little reason for them to stay.

The small man stepped up to Sam and ran his hands down his sides feeling for a gun. Finding none, he moved back and glanced at the big one. He said. "The dude ain't heeled, Smoky, but that don't prove nothing. I figger McHale's lying about this hombre being Cassidy's boy. Sure looks like a sheepman to me."

The big man nodded. He rubbed a hand over his bearded face, scratched the back of his neck, and nodded again. "He even smells like a sheepman. I don't reckon we oughta let him go into town and stink up all that good cowmen air."

The small man grinned and motioned back up the road toward Tremont Pass. "Start walking, sonny." He stepped to the edge of the road. "Get out of the way, Smoky. Let's not keep McHale from going into town."

These were the kind of men Sam instinctively hated, but to be called a sheepman was an insult that would have sent his temper skyrocketing if they had been solid citizens. Even if it meant getting his head shot off, he knew he was going to rush these men, that he was incapable of turning around and obeying them.

He stood motionlessly for a few seconds as the small man's gaze turned to the big one. Just as Sam tensed his body to lunge at the small man, his fists swinging, McHale snapped his whip within an inch of Smoky's right ear making it crack like a pistol shot. The fellow jumped and let out a yell. In that exact instant Sam reached the small man, grabbed the wrist of his gun hand, and twisted the revolver from his fingers. He tossed the .45 into the brush below the road, then knocked the man into the dust with a sledging blow to his jaw.

Smoky tried to line his gun on Sam, but he had come so close to losing his right ear that he had been momentarily paralyzed. He moved slowly and Sam was on him before he could pull the trigger.

Sam threw a right to the side of the man's head, then drove a left into his belly. Smoky tottered back, weaving uncertainly on his feet, a hand coming to his stomach as he struggled to suck air back into his tortured lungs. His right hand that held his gun dropped to his side. Sam hit him on the side of his face again. The big man's knees buckled and he went down in a slow, curling fall, the revolver falling to the ground.

Sam picked up the revolver and tossed it as far as he could into the brush, then he rolled the man off the edge of the road and watched him slide down the steep slope, raising a cloud of dust and creating a small avalanche of rocks and dirt.

"Look out!" McHale yelled.

Sam wheeled as the small man lunged at him, a knife in his hand. Stepping to one side, Sam threw out a foot and tripped him. The fellow sprawled on the ground, his momentum carrying him forward so that he slid on his belly, his chin digging into the dirt like a sled runner. Sam picked him up by the belt and his shirt collar and heaved him over the edge of the road. He turned to the stage, climbed to the seat, and said: "Let her roll, Buck."

McHale released the brake, threw out the silk with the usual sharp, pistol-like report, and the coach wheeled on down the road. He looked at Sam and shook his head admiringly. "You never even raised a sweat. I wish Ben Faraday could have seen the way you handled them toughs."

"I wish Monk Corley could have seen it." Sam was still so angry he had trouble keeping his voice under control. "I'm going to ask Ben for that star. I aim to make Monk sorry he ever sent for those yahoos."

"I was watching you," McHale said, "and I seen the back of your neck getting red. I knowed you had one hell of a temper, so I figured you was fixing to jump 'em. Did you stop to think they might have killed you?"

Sam nodded, his hands clenched on his lap. "I know I did a fool thing, Buck. I broke one of the basic rules Ben drilled into me last summer. I can't think of anything more stupid than jumping two men with guns in their hands, but I couldn't help it. They said I smelled like a sheepman."

McHale nodded. "I wouldn't have stood still for it, neither."

"It doesn't make sense," Sam said. "They knew I wasn't a hardcase that Black Mike Nickels had sent for."

"Oh, they knowed who you was, all right," McHale said, "so you might ask your pa why Monk Corley didn't want you to come home. Or maybe Jonas don't want you back hisself."

"No, it wasn't Pa," Sam said. "There's nothing sly about him. He'd have come right out and said so if he didn't want me to come home. Monk must have his own reason. Now will you tell me what the ruckus is all about?"

They were at the edge of the scattered timber, the grass-covered hills stretching for miles in front of them. They could see Cañon, still so far away that it looked like a toy town set among the cotton-woods on the bank of Cañon Creek.

McHale pointed to a small pine beside the road. A sign was nailed to the trunk. Even from a distance Sam could read the tall, black letters: NO SHEEP ALLOWED PAST THIS POINT.

"Corley and the rest of the cowmen have run a deadline from Mount Grizzly south to Cold Springs," McHale said. "The ruckus started when Black Mike said he was gonna push his sheep out into the grass. He's been penned up in the mountains and on Dutchman Flat ever since he started raising sheep twenty years ago. I guess now that he's got three grown boys and some money saved, he figgers it's time to make his move."

"He's asking for trouble," Sam said thoughtfully, "but he's been a taxpayer and a citizen of Cañon County for more than twenty years. He's got a right to some of the good grass. I hate sheep, but the cowmen don't have any legal authority to mark off a deadline."

"That's what Black Mike claims," McHale said, "but it ain't the whole story. Mike went to the Cattlemen's Association last spring and asked 'em fair and square for a chunk of the valley grass. He said he'd see his sheep stayed inside the boundaries they gave him. He's got too many for Dutchman Flat and the mountain pasture he's used all this time. Corley and his bunch turned Mike down and said he'd have to sell part of his band. They wouldn't give him a blade of grass more'n he's got."

"So he boiled over," Sam said.

"Yeah, you can say that," McHale agreed, "only you'd never guess what he said he'd do. He sent for Dale Sontag to fetch in three bands of sheep from Utah. That's why Corley put them two hardcases out here on the road. You know what Sontag is."

Sam nodded. He knew, all right. Dale Sontag was a ruthless Utah sheepman who kept a crew of gunslingers on his payroll and used them to open up new pasture for his sheep. If he invaded Cañon County, he'd trigger a range war that would take lives and cause more misery than all the grass in the state was worth.

Sam considered it the rest of the way into town; he thought about Kitty Nickels, too, Black Mike's daughter. Sam and Kitty had been in love as far back as their high school days. She was, he admitted, the magnet that had brought him back to Cañon.

Sam wanted to get married at once. Judging from Kitty's last letter, she was willing, but a range war would put them on opposite sides. He hadn't heard from her for more than a week, and now he wondered if this was the reason. Maybe she wouldn't even meet the stage.

II

When the coach stopped in front of the Cañon Hotel, the usual crowd was on hand to see who had come to town. Sam stepped down, noting that his mother was the only one who was here to meet him. She came to him a little timidly, for he had never been one to encourage a public show of affection, but today was different. These last months in Laramie had been long and hard and lonely. He swept his mother into his arms and hugged her and kissed her, then he pushed her back and looked at her and at the same time sneaked a second glance at the crowd to see if he had missed Kitty Nickels when he had looked before, but he was certain now she wasn't here.

"You're looking fine, Ma," Sam said. "You're getting younger every day instead of older."

She laughed and patted his cheek. "Oh, go on now, Samuel," she said, pleased. "I can't say the same about you. You're tired, aren't you?"

"The finals were tough," he said, not wanting to tell her about his brush with Monk Corley's men. "I made it, though. I've got my sheepskin in my trunk. We'll nail it up over the fireplace so Dad can brag about it to everybody who comes into the house."

"He will, too," she said. "He's sorry he couldn't meet the stage, but he couldn't get away from the bank just now. He wants you to come right over. I'll go home and start supper, and you go to the bank. He's got something important to talk to you about."

Sam didn't say anything because he would only hurt his mother, but the old, familiar resentment rose in him again. Maybe it had never left. He often wondered if it had started that night twenty-two years ago when he was born and his father had looked at him and said to Doc Harvey: "How can a little, shriveled-up thing like that ever amount to a damn?"

Doc had told it a dozen times afterward in Sam's hearing and laughed as if it were funny. It was never funny to Sam who suspected that Jonas Cassidy had felt the same way ever since. The making of money for the sake of having money had never appealed to Sam, but to his father it was the only standard to decide whether a man amounted to anything.

"All right, Ma," Sam said. "I'll leave my valises in the hotel lobby and go on over to the bank."

"You hurry now," she said anxiously. "Pa's expecting you right away."

Mrs. Cassidy started to turn, then paused when Sam asked: "Have you seen Kitty lately?"

Mrs. Cassidy's mouth firmed out, the fingers clutching her reticule turned white. She said slowly: "Kitty's fine. I saw her this morning, but she told me she couldn't meet the stage. Her father and the twins are in town. Don't you go over there, Sam. You'll just get into a fight if you do."

"Why Ma," he said, grinning, "you know I never started a fight in my life."

"Maybe not," she said, "but you do seem to attract them. Now you go on over to the bank."

"All right, Ma," he said.

Buck McHale had rolled the stage on down the street. As soon as Mrs. Cassidy left, the men who knew Sam and had held back out of courtesy to his mother moved up and shook hands and told him they were glad to see him. Bill Barton who owned the livery stable, Doc Harvey, Charley Knowles who ran the drugstore, and even Morry Jacks, the town drunk—all slapped him on the back and told him it had been a dull winter, but they expected things to liven up now that he was home. After they drifted away, Sam picked up his valises and stepped into the lobby and set them down close to the wall. As he straightened up, he saw Sheriff Ben Faraday was waiting to shake hands.

"I'm mighty glad to see you, Sam," Faraday said. "I wanted to talk to you as soon as your ma left, but then everybody else had to have a whack at you." He glanced at the clock on the wall above Hoby Stewart, the hotel clerk. "I heard your ma tell you to go see Jonas, but you've got a few minutes before he locks the front door of the bank. What I've got to say won't wait."

"I'm glad to see you, Ben," Sam said as he shook hands. "I'm glad to be home, too. The truth is I just wasn't cut out to be a scholar."

Faraday grinned around his cigar and motioned toward the black leather chairs set against the far wall of the lobby. "Let's sit over yonder," he said. As they crossed the room to the chairs, he added in a low tone: "I didn't want Hoby to hear what I've got to say. His sickness is getting worse."

"Sickness?" Sam glanced at the bald-headed little clerk who was listening as hard as he could while pretending to be busy. "What's the matter with him?"

"Constipation of the mind and diarrhea of the mouth," Faraday said. "He's had it for years, but, like I said, he's getting worse."

Sam laughed as he dropped into one of the chairs. He looked at the clock again and saw that he had less than fifteen minutes to get to the bank. Rebellion was mixed with bitterness now as he wondered why his father couldn't take five minutes from his penny counting to meet the stage. But he never had, so Sam guessed he had no reason to think today would be different.

He drew tobacco and paper from his vest pocket and rolled a

smoke. Faraday sat down beside him, but he was restless and got up at once. His cigar had gone out. He relit it, his moody gaze on the front of the bank across the street.

Faraday might be fifty, or sixty. Sam couldn't guess, although right now he would have said sixty or older. The sheriff had aged a great deal in the months since Sam had been home. For years the sheriff's mustache and hair had been white, but he'd always had a young look about him, the look of a man who was ageless and could handle any problem that came along. Now the lines showed around his eyes and in his cheeks. His back, which had always been as straight as the barrel of his .45, was bent a little, as if he now lacked the strength to stand as erectly as he always had before.

The silence ribboned out. Sam shot a glance at the clock again and wondered why Faraday didn't start talking. Then, the sheriff wheeled from the window and asked: "What are you going to do, Sam?"

"Read law in Judge Murray's office," Sam answered. "Pa doesn't know it yet and he'll yell like a wounded bull when I tell him, but he'll just have to yell."

Faraday nodded as if he knew this was what Sam would say. He yanked a copy of the Cañon County *Gazette* out of a coat pocket and pointed to a small article on the front page that was framed in black.

"Read it," Faraday said.

Sam took the paper and read:

WARNING: The Cañon County Sheep Shooters Association warns all sheepmen to keep their bands from crossing the deadline that is clearly marked. Do not disregard this warning.

"I suppose Buck McHale was happy to pass along the word that hell's busted loose since you were home?" Faraday said.

Sam nodded. "I had a taste of it myself." He told Faraday about his trouble with the two toughs, and added: "I've got a lecture coming, Ben. Seems that I forgot everything you taught me."

"I'm the one who's got the lecture coming," Faraday said bitterly. "Hell, I could've got you killed."

"You?"

"Yeah, me. I've told several people I was waiting to appoint a deputy after you got home on account of I was hoping you'd take the job. Looks to me like Monk Corley didn't want you toting the deputy's star. I don't blame him, neither. I don't have much skookum left, and Monk could handle most of the men I might appoint, but he knows damned well he can't handle you."

"If you're offering me the star, I'll take it," Sam said. "Reading law can wait a while. I aim to make Monk Corley ..."

"Now, hold on a minute," Faraday broke in. "I ain't offering you a star just so you can make Corley crawl. I don't want you to get yourself killed, neither." He took the newspaper from Sam. "We hadn't heard a word about no Sheep Shooters Association, but it sounds like more of Corley's doings. I don't suppose they'll murder any men, but they'll shoot some sheep, all right, and Black Mike has got his dander up to where he won't back down. I dunno when he aims to make his move, but his sheep are right up next to the deadline now."

"Ma said Mike and the twins were in town."

Faraday nodded. "They came in to buy supplies and ammunition. Pete's with the sheep. It's my guess Mike and the twins will be back with the band before morning. Come sunup, they'll move 'em across the deadline."

"What about Dale Sontag?" Sam asked.

"He ain't showed up yet," Faraday said. "I heard Sontag won't start till Black Mike has crossed the deadline. If he gets away with it, then Sontag will come in."

"It doesn't sound much like him," Sam said.

"I dunno," Faraday said. "He's smart, and he ain't as young as he was once, so maybe he ain't hankering for a fight like he used to. But if he does come, we've got big trouble."

Sam nodded agreement, wondering what Faraday's private feelings were. He was a cowman and he hated sheep, but he was a stickler for law and order, and Monk Corley and the self-styled Sheep Shooters Association would ignore the law just as they had ignored it with the deadline.

Cañon County had always been cattle country with the exception of Black Mike Nickels' sheep. He had been left alone because he had stayed in the mountains and on Dutchman Flat that was not far from his home ranch at Two Springs. Sam had hoped it wouldn't change. His father felt the same. The bank had always loaned money to the cowmen, but never to Black Mike Nickels. That was one of the reasons Mike viewed Jonas Cassidy with a deep and passionate hatred.

Sam looked at the clock again and rose. "I've got to go."

"Wait," Faraday said. "There's one more thing before you decide about taking the star ..."

"I've decided," Sam said.

"You listen now," Faraday said sharply. "I'm sick, Sam. I've got something growing in me. Doc says I've got two, three months. Six at the most. Maybe I'll still be alive at election time. I was hoping you'd take the deputy's star and run for sheriff come November. But what you've got to understand is that I won't be much help. I'll back any play you make, but my hard riding days are over. You're young and you'll be criticized. You figure you can take it?"

"I'm sorry to hear this," Sam said, shocked. "Maybe Doc's wrong. He can make a mistake ..."

"He didn't," Faraday said. "You still want the star?"

"I want it," Sam said.

"Good. The job pays seventy-five dollars a month, and you'll get twenty-five dollars more for serving as town marshal. Now go see your pa, then come to my office and I'll give you the star."

A hundred a month was enough to get married on, Sam thought. He didn't know whether Kitty would approve or not, but he hoped she would because he was going to take the job.

"I'll be there, Ben," he said.

He left the lobby on the run, hearing the clock strike as he went through the door.

III

Sam reached the bank just as his father was letting Monk Corley out. It was that close. Another minute and Jonas Cassidy would have had the door locked. Sam, knowing how obstinate his father was, felt certain that he could have pounded on it until his knuckles were raw but the door would have stayed locked.

Corley paused, his pale blue eyes fixed on Sam, a shocked expression on his dark face for just a moment, then it passed and he assumed an air of friendliness as he held out his big hand.

"How are you, Sam?" Corley asked in his ringing voice of authority. "I heard you were coming home today."

"I'm sure you did," Sam said as he shook hands. "I guess you're a little surprised to see me."

Corley scratched his head, pretending that he didn't understand what Sam meant. He was a big man, tall and broad of shoulder, a man who dominated Cañon County partly through the sheer power of his personality and partly through wealth. His MC was the biggest spread in the valley, his range running from the summit of the Bearpaws through the foothills and on into the desert. He was brutal and physically powerful, but for some reason his men loved him. Sam didn't know why. As far as he could see, Monk Corley was the most unlovable of men. Perhaps it was because he often said he never asked his men to do anything he wouldn't. This, Sam knew, was not an idle boast.

"Why no, I'm not surprised," Corley said.

"I believe you are," Sam said hotly. "You posted a couple of hard-cases up there on this side of the pass who were supposed to turn back any gunslingers Black Mike Nickels was bringing in. They claimed I was a sheepman and they were going to make me walk back over the pass while Buck McHale brought the stage into Cañon."

"I did post a couple of men up there," Corley said. "Everyone in town knows that, Jonas included, but I didn't expect them to turn you back. "What makes you think I had anything to do with a mistake like that?"

"Any damned fool could tell I'm not a sheepman," Sam said, his anger growing. "I've been insulted in a lot of ways, but that's one I'm not taking from anybody."

Jonas had been standing in the doorway, his face getting red as he listened. Now he said in the clipped way he had of talking to Sam when he was highly irritated: "I think you owe Monk an apology, Sam."

"Never mind an apology," Corley said quickly. "I'll talk to those boys. You're right, Sam. It was an insult." He started to turn away, then swung back. "I'm curious how you got here if they were making you walk back over the pass."

"I took their guns away from them," Sam said. "You'd better go see about them. I hope I broke their damned necks."

An expression of incredulity was on Corley's face. "Oh, come on, Sam," he said. "You know who those men were?"

"I don't know and I don't care," Sam said, "but I'll tell you one thing, Monk. I'm going to be wearing my gun as soon as I can get my hands on it. If they ever poke their heads into view down here in Cañon, I'll shoot 'em off."

"I'll pass the word and it'll scare hell out of 'em," Corley said. "So long, Jonas."

He strode along the walk toward O'Hara's Bar. Sam stared at the big man's broad back, knowing that he might have to carry out the threat he'd made, and knowing, too, that Monk Corley didn't believe a word he'd said. Well, Corley could think he was a liar if he wanted to. After he'd had a talk with those two plug-uglies, he'd rate Sam a little higher in his book.

"Come in, Samuel," Jonas said in the same clipped way he'd spoken before.

Sam stepped inside the bank and heard the click of the lock behind him. His father was sore, but rebellion was so high in Sam he didn't care. Jonas Cassidy could kowtow to Monk Corley till hell froze over, but his boy Samuel wouldn't.

Jonas turned and walked into his private office in the rear of the building, his leather heels tapping sharply on the floor. Sam hesitated, hoping his anger would cool. He wanted to avoid a quarrel with his father if he could. As he pushed back the swinging gate at the end of the counter, he saw that the cashier, Bob Darrow, was not in the teller's cage. Sam was surprised because at this time of day Darrow was usually counting his money and going over the checks he had cashed since the bank had opened at 9:00 that morning. Harry Pierce, the bookkeeper, was seated on his tall stool working on a ledger, his green eyeshade pulled low on his forehead.

Sam swung to one side and offered his hand to Pierce, saying in a low tone: "I'll bet the books still show a profit."

Pierce was a bachelor, a tall, skinny man who had worked here for years. Sam often wondered why he stayed. He was capable, and he could have found work somewhere else that paid more than Jonas did, but apparently he liked the prestige that came from working in a bank.

"They show a profit, all right," Pierce said as he shook hands. "If they didn't, your pa would cut my salary."

"I guess he'd be looking for a new bookkeeper if he did that," Sam said.

"Oh no, I'd go right on working for him if I had to pay him for the privilege," Pierce said with a straight face, then he smiled as he added: "I'm glad to see you back, son."

"I'm glad to be back, Harry," Sam said, and went on into his father's office.

Jonas stood behind the desk, waiting for Sam to come in, his face showing his annoyance. He was a full head shorter than Sam, a precise man who wore a black mustache that was always perfectly trimmed just as his hair was perfectly cut and always in place. Jonas Cassidy had a sharp, incisive mind and an uncanny business sense. He had started to work for another man in this very bank and within a few years had owned it. He was always impatient with Sam, or so it seemed, and he was obviously impatient now.

When Sam sat down, he felt the tension that seemed to tighten every nerve in his body. For several years he had felt this tension whenever he was alone with his father. He pondered this as he waited for Jonas to take a cigar from the box in front of him, bite off the end, and light it, the usual ritual before the talk started.

Sam had never felt this tension with anyone else, not even with his most difficult teachers when he was in college. Maybe it had something to do with making money that had never been important to him, but was and always had been the complete and total purpose of life to his father. Or possibly just now it was because his father hated to have to wait, although he constantly made other people wait.

Sam slumped back in the chair and straightened his long legs in front of him. He could wait as long as his father could. Right now Jonas Cassidy seemed to be in no hurry as he played with his cigar. He turned it between his fingers and started at it, apparently determined to make Sam nervous. Suddenly the thought occurred to Sam that his father was the epitome of the hackneyed jokes and sayings that were prevalent about small town bankers. He felt an almost compulsive desire to laugh, but he controlled it, knowing what would happen if he let himself go.

"I didn't get to where I am by insulting men of Monk Corley's stature," Jonas said at last.

Sam came close to saying he didn't want to get to the place his father was, but he restrained himself. Instead, he said: "I didn't insult him. It was his men who insulted me."

Jonas studied his cigar for a few more seconds, then he raised his gaze to Sam's face. "I asked your mother to tell you to come to the bank as soon as you got in," he said.

"She told me."

"Why didn't you?"

Sam hesitated, then he said: "I thought that if there was any real hurry about seeing me, you would have met the stage. After all, it was just a matter of crossing the street."

Few people had the temerity to question Jonas Cassidy's actions. Sam wasn't sure that he had ever done it before, but he knew what was ahead, and he thought he'd better start breaking the ice. If this interview meant a final and irrevocable break between him and Jonas Cassidy, then so be it. He was his own man and this was the time to make it plain.

Jonas blinked, took another bite on his cigar, and actually flushed. "I was busy," he said. "I was having an important conference with Monk Corley."

"Then I guess I would have waited," Sam said.

"Yes, I suppose you would have."

"I would have come sooner," Sam said, "but I ran into Ben Faraday. He wanted to talk to me."

"That has-been?" Jonas dismissed Faraday with a wave of a slim-fingered hand. "He's coming up for election this fall, but we've got to find a new man. Ben's getting old and he's failed a lot the last few months."

"He offered me a job."

Jonas laughed. "I suppose he thinks you'll go back to riding for him at thirty dollars a month again. Well, you're a college man now with a business education. You'll be an asset to the bank. I let Bob Darrow go last month. The job will pay you fifty dollars a month ..."

"But Bob had been in the bank for ten years or more," Sam said. "You couldn't just let him go like that."

"Why not?" Jonas asked, amused. "I'll be happy to have my son in business with me. As a matter of fact, I've been looking forward to it. I never was really satisfied to go off and leave Bob here to make decisions. His judgment in business matters was faulty, but you'll soon learn anything you need to know. There are times when people ask for loans and I have to look at a herd of cattle or a piece of property."

Sam straightened in his chair and leaned forward. "Dad, did you ever ask me if I wanted to work in the bank?"

"No," Jonas said, surprised. "I've always assumed that you would. That's why I sent you to college."

It was true, Sam knew. Probably the only motive his father had was just what he had said, that a college man would be an asset to the bank.

"You should have asked me before you let Bob Darrow go," Sam said. "I can't work in a bank, penned up in a teller's cage all day. I've made arrangements to read law in Judge Murray's office, but that will be later. Right now I'm taking the deputy's star."

Jonas took the cigar from his mouth. It probably would have fallen out if he hadn't. He sat as if paralyzed, his eyes wide and filled with disbelief. Then he said harshly: "By God, I paid for your education. Good, hard money. I expect a return on it."

Sam rose. He had known the interview would go this way, but now that it had, he found the tension more than he could bear. He said: "Add up all the money you've spent for my education and give the bill to me. I'll repay you with interest."

"I didn't mean you had to do that," Jonas said. "All I want is for you to work for me. Is that too much to ask?"

"Yes, that's too much," Sam said. "I've got to live my own

life and I've got to pick the kind of work I think I can do. There's another thing. I hope to marry Kitty Nickels. I can't do it on fifty dollars a month."

Jonas jammed his cigar into an ashtray, his face turning white. "I won't let you marry the daughter of that sheepherder. You'd have my blessing with any other girl in the county, but you'll never marry her."

"Then I'll have to marry her without your blessing," Sam said, and wheeled toward the door.

"We'll talk about the job tonight at supper," Jonas called after him.

Sam didn't stop or look back. He strode out of the office, pushed back the gate at the end of the counter, and went on to the front door. He unlocked it and, opening it, stepped outside and pulled it shut behind him. He was breathing hard from suppressed anger. He wondered if the time would ever come when his father would stop trying to dictate his life.

He crossed to the hotel. Morry Jacks, the town drunk, was leaning against the wall. He winked at Sam, asking: "Gonna be a banker just like your old man?"

"No, I'm not." Sam dug 50¢ out of his pants pocket and gave it to Jacks. "Morry, I've got a couple of things to do before supper. Would you carry my valises home and tell Ma I may be late?"

"Sure," Morry said as he took the coin. "Glad to help out."

Sam walked away. He started toward the courthouse to get the deputy's star from Ben Faraday, then changed his mind and turned the corner. The Nickels house was in the next block. He had to see Kitty to find out why she hadn't met him. If he had to fight the twins, or Black Mike himself, he'd do it, but he was going to see Kitty.

IV

The Nickels house with its mansard roof and green shutters was one of the two finest in Cañon, the Cassidy home at the opposite end of town being the other. Black Mike and the twins spent most of their time on the ranch, coming to town usually only on special occasions such as Christmas, the Fourth of July, and the fair in the fall. But they were here now, all right, the three of them standing on the porch, great hulking men who had the reputation of being the best barroom brawlers in the county.

Sam opened the gate in the picket fence, stepped through it, then closed it, noting that it squealed as loudly as it had the last time he had been here. He turned slowly from it to face the men on the porch, saying: "I don't think you've oiled those hinges since Christmas, Mike."

Black Mike Nickels' face was a thundercloud. He said: "You ain't welcome here and you know it. Now git."

"I sure didn't come to see you, Mike," Sam said. "I want to see Kitty. Where is she?"

Black Mike jerked a thumb toward the open front door. "She's in the kitchen doing the work a woman's supposed to do. We knowed you were coming in on the stage today and I told her she wasn't leaving the house to meet the likes of you. I told you once and I won't tell you again. Git."

Sam shook his head. "I'm going to marry Kitty, Mike, if she'll have me, and I think she will. You've run roughshod over your family as long as I've known you. If your boys want to stand for it, that's their business, but Kitty doesn't have to. Tell her I'm here."

For a moment Black Mike stood motionlessly, his big hands clenched at his sides, his dark eyes fixed on Sam's face, the corners of his mouth working as he fought his temper. Sam was certain the man had nothing against him personally. He had been condemned on the grounds that he was Jonas Cassidy's son, and Jonas Cassidy was on the side of the cowmen. It was as simple as that, and the unfairness of it made Sam furious.

"Damn it, I'm not responsible for what my father or Monk Corley or any of the cowmen have done," Sam said. "This is between me and Kitty, and you've got no right to stand against us. She's over eighteen. If she wants to keep house for me instead of you, it's her business."

"You've been warned!" Black Mike bellowed. "Get him, Shawn. Throw him into the street."

One of the twins came down off the porch in a great jump, letting out a bellow of anticipation as he hit the ground. He was three inches taller than Sam and twenty pounds heavier; he had tremendous arms and shoulders, and it was his way to take a punch on the jaw in order to get in close enough to get his arms around his victim and hug him. Shawn could break a man's ribs with his grip. That was the Nickels' way of fighting; Black Mike had always fought that way and he had taught his sons to do the same. Sam knew it, but he stood his ground. With perfect timing he threw a right into Shawn's belly, a powerful blow that drove wind out of the twin and stopped him in his tracks. Again Sam's timing was perfect as he brought his left through to Shawn's jaw, snapping his big head back and sending him sprawling.

"Get up!" Black Mike raged. "What the hell's the matter with you? I told you to throw him out, not lie down and take a nap."

But Shawn didn't move. He'd been knocked cold. Sam rubbed his knuckles against his shirt. "Your boy has a hard jaw, Mike," he said. "Now will you tell Kitty I'm here before I break some bones in my hand?"

"By God, Rory!" Black Mike shouted in a voice that trembled with rage, "he can't be lucky again. Throw him into the street and give him a kick in the ribs for Shawn while's he's down."

Rory came down off the porch in exactly the same way Shawn had and charged Sam with his great arms extended as his brother had done. He had learned nothing from what had happened to Shawn. It was the only way he knew how to fight and, apparently like his father, considered it sheer luck that Sam had knocked Shawn out. The same thing happened. Sam rammed his right fist into Rory's belly and hammered the wind out of him. He stood motionless for an instant, a pained expression on his face as he struggled to suck air into his lungs. Sam threw his left to young Nickels' jaw. Rory sprawled beside Shawn and lay still.

"They both have hard jaws, Mike." Sam rubbed his knuckles on his shirt again and shook his head. "I did a little boxing in Laramie, Mike. I forgot to tell you. I took a few beatings, but I did learn to throw a punch. You want to try it now?"

Black Mike stared at his two boys, lying flat on their backs in the grass side-by-side. Slowly he raised his head and stared at Sam. He said with grudging respect: "I reckon it ain't just luck when you do it twice in a row like that. No, I don't want to try it."

"Then will you please tell Kitty that I'm here and that I want to—" Sam began.

He stopped. There was no need to go on. Kitty had rushed out through the front door. Now she stopped and stared at her brothers who were beginning to stir, then whirled on her father. "I told you to let me know if Sam came to see me. I told you not to ..." She paused and turned to look at her brothers and burst out laughing. "Sam, that's about as comical a sight as I ever looked at in my life.

They've had it coming for a long time, but they never met up with anyone who was man enough to do it before."

"All I did was to ask to see you," Sam said.

"That's enough," Black Mike snapped. "All right, you've seen her, Cassidy. Now git."

The boys were sitting up, both rubbing their jaws and glaring at Sam. "Where'd you hide that club you were carrying?" Shawn demanded. "I didn't even see you hit me with it."

"I didn't use a club," Sam said. "Just my fist."

"You're a liar," Rory said. "Nobody can hit a man like that with just his fist."

"I'm afraid he's telling the truth," Black Mike said. "I sure never learned you boys much about scrapping. This college fellow walks in and knocks both of you bowlegged." He gave Kitty a push toward the door. "Git back inside and tend to your chores. Sooner or later Cassidy's gonna git it through his skull that he ain't gonna see you, and then maybe he'll have sense enough to pull his freight."

Kitty stepped back, her dark eyes scornful. She had the Nickels' temper and her father's coloring, his black hair and dark eyes, but that was as far as the resemblance went. She was slim-bodied, quick-moving, and graceful, and, in Sam's opinion, she was a very pretty girl. How she could have been sired by a man like Black Mike was more than Sam had ever been able to understand.

Sam's first reaction when Black Mike gave Kitty a shove was to haul him off the porch and give him the same treatment he'd given the twins, but he saw that wasn't necessary. Kitty could take care of herself.

She backed toward the door, saying angrily: "I've cooked and scrubbed and kept this house so you'd have a place in town to come to when you wanted it, and I've looked after Pete while he was in high school. I've earned the right to entertain my company in my own parlor." She turned to face Sam. "Come in. We'll sit on the couch and you can do your courting, fit and proper."

"No he don't!" Black Mike bellowed. "If you take him into the house, you can get out. You won't have no home with me if you're bound and determined to see this man."

"I'm bound and determined," she snapped. "If that's the way it is, I'm leaving. Wait for me, Sam."

She ran into the house. Sam didn't move, but he watched the twins out of the corners of his eyes without appearing to, not at all sure they'd stay where they were, but they did, apparently having had all the fighting they wanted for the day. Black Mike's face had turned a dark red, a pulse pounded in his forehead, but he didn't even move when Kitty came out of the house with a suitcase.

"I'm sorry for you, Pa," Kitty said. "It doesn't have to be this way."

Still Black Mike didn't move or say a word as she went down the steps and handed her suitcase to Sam. They walked along the path to the gate. He opened it. Kitty moved through it. He followed her, and shut the gate behind them. They turned toward the business block. Sam was carrying the suitcase in his left hand, his right gripping her left.

The story of what had happened would be all over town in a matter of minutes, or some garbled version of it. He had given the people of Cañon enough to talk about for the next week, and he hadn't been in town two hours. But he didn't care. He glanced at Kitty and saw that she was looking straight down the street, her head held high. He noticed that she did not look back once.

V

Sam and Kitty went into the hotel lobby together. She signed the register. Hoby Stewart gave her a key, and Sam climbed the stairs with her. Stewart stared at them, pop-eyed. This, too, Sam thought, would be all over town in a matter of minutes.

As soon as they were in her room, Sam put her suitcase down and she fled into his arms. He held her against his chest and let her cry. When she was able to stop, she wiped her eyes and turned from him and walked to the window to stare into the street.

"It wasn't enough for Pa to fight the cowmen," she said, "after he's been getting along all right for years. It isn't enough to send for Dale Sontag and have him bring in gunmen who'll come to Cañon and kill men we've known all our lives." She swallowed, and added: "He's got to take it out on me and you, too."

"Marry me," Sam said. "Tomorrow. I love you, Kitty. I came close to quitting school more than once last winter to come home and ask you to marry me. I'd have stayed here and gotten a job if you had said yes. Well, I didn't quit and now I've got a job. There's no reason why we shouldn't get married."

She turned from the window to look at him. She tried to smile, but the smile wouldn't come. "I love you, Sam," she said softly. "You know that. I need you very much, but we both know we can't get married tomorrow."

"I'd like to know why," he said.

"As long as you're working for your father ..."

"I'm not," he cut in. "I aim to study law like I told you in my last letter, but that will have to wait. I'm going to be Ben Faraday's deputy."

"No, honey." She ran to him and put her hands on his arms. "You can't do that. You'll get yourself killed and for what? There's other men who can do things like that. Go ahead and read law in Judge Murray's office. Start in the morning."

"Who is there in this county who can do things like that besides me?" Sam asked. "Maybe I'm bragging, but at least I've had a little experience. Besides, Ben trusts me. I'm not on either side, though folks probably won't believe that." He frowned, thinking about himself and Monk Corley, and added: "There's another thing. I guess I'm selfish, but I want to whittle Corley down. There will never be any peace or justice in this county until somebody does."

She sighed. "All right, Sam. I knew there wasn't any use to argue with you about it." She shook her head. "Maybe you'll have to cut Pa down to size, too. He's as bull-headed and short-sighted as Corley. Like leaving Pete out there by himself with the sheep. Tomorrow he's aiming to cross the deadline. Everybody knows that. He's publicly announced it. If he wants to get killed, I guess that's his business. Shawn and Rory are old enough to figure their chances and to know what may happen to them, but Pete isn't. He may be the one to get killed."

Sam nodded, knowing it was true. He asked: "You want me to go out there and talk to him?"

She shook her head. "Not tonight. Maybe tomorrow. Let's wait and see. If Pa keeps on the way he's going and Corley keeps on, there'd bound to be a collision and a lot of men are going to get killed. All we can do now is to hope that something will happen to stop it."

"I've got to go," he said. "I need to see Ben Faraday. Do you have any money?"

She shook her head. "Not a cent. That was one way Pa kept us in line."

He dug into his pocket and drew out all the money he had. "It's not much," he said, "but it'll keep you going for a while. Maybe I can borrow some from Ben."

She hesitated, then took the money, her gaze on the floor. "I'll find a job, Sam. I don't know what, but I'll find something to do and I'll pay you back."

"Not if I can talk you into marrying me first," he said.

He kissed her, and he knew then how much she needed him and depended upon him. When she finally let him go, she turned quickly from him and walked back to the window. "I'll see you in the morning," he said, and left the room.

As Sam walked through the lobby, he saw that Hoby Stewart was watching him with a knowing grin on his face. Sam's fists knotted and he had to fight an impulse to turn back to the desk and wipe the grin off the clerk's face, but he didn't give way to the impulse. He had or would have enough enemies in Cañon without adding to them.

He went directly to Ben Faraday's cabin, which was across a side street from the courthouse. The sheriff lived there by himself when he was in town, but it was no secret that he preferred staying on his ranch. He asked Sam in and, picking up a star from the table, pinned it on Sam's shirt.

"I guess that was what you came after, wasn't it?" Faraday asked.

"You're a mind reader," Sam said.

Faraday had been having supper. Sam glanced at the table and saw that the sheriff had been eating nothing except crackers and tea. Sam remembered what Faraday had told him about something growing inside him. Maybe it was true. The sheriff had always been a hearty eater. He was a sick man or he wouldn't be eating a meal like this.

"No, not a mind reader," Faraday said. "All I knew was what I kept hoping would happen. I thought I'd better get this star pinned onto you before you changed your mind."

"I wasn't likely to change my mind," Sam said, and told him about his fight with the Nickels boys and Kitty's leaving home.

Faraday sat down as if he were too tired to keep standing. He said: "Black Mike is a fool, but there's no use talking to him. I've tried. Kitty's right about Pete. I'll ride out there with you in the morning."

"If you don't feel like it ..." Sam began.

"No, I don't feel like it," Faraday said, "but I'm going to anyway. If I give up, I'll be in a rocking chair or flat in bed the rest of my life. I couldn't stand it even if it was only for a little while."

Sam nodded, knowing Faraday well enough to understand what he meant. If he were helpless, it would be the most galling experience in his life. He had always been an independent man, the kind who would shoot himself before he lived as a complete invalid.

"I'll see you first thing in the morning," Sam said, "and we'll ride out to the sheep camp."

On his way home, he thought about the ancient argument over what would happen if an irresistible force met an immovable object. That was just about what would happen when Black Mike Nickels moved his sheep across the deadline. The real tragedy was that innocent people like young Pete Nickels would be caught when the collision took place. For a moment Sam played with the thought of riding out to the sheep camp after supper, but gave it up. He and Faraday would be there early in the morning and that would be soon enough. There was no reason for anything to happen tonight. Whatever countermove Monk Corley planned would come after the sheep had crossed the deadline.

Sam walked into the Cassidy house five minutes after six, which had been the supper hour as long as he could remember. Not one minute till six or one minute after six, but exactly six. Mrs. Cassidy had put up with this kind of precise timing all of her married life and she had never, as far as Sam knew, raised an objection. Tonight they had waited supper for Sam. When he stepped into the front room after hanging his hat on the hall tree, he found Jonas pacing back and forth. His father said harshly: "Go upstairs and wash. You have already delayed supper five minutes."

Sam went upstairs, thinking that if he could not persuade Kitty to marry him, he would have to move into the hotel. To Jonas Cassidy he was still a boy of ten. Perhaps he always would be. He knew one thing. He could not live the way his mother did.

He washed in the bathroom, the only bathroom in Cañon. Black Mike Nickels might have as fine a house as Jonas Cassidy, but he didn't have a bathroom, a fact in which Jonas took smug satisfaction.

When he came downstairs, Jonas was seated at the head of the table and Mrs. Cassidy was setting dishes of hot food in front of him. Sam sat down in his usual chair on the side, his mother taking the chair at the foot a moment later. His father gave the blessing and began helping himself. He ignored the star on Sam's shirt, though it was a thing he could hardly have overlooked.

Mrs. Cassidy made a few casual remarks about the weather, but her efforts to start a conversation were futile. Jonas maintained a sullen silence, letting his expression indicate that he was displeased at having his supper delayed. When the chocolate cake was finished, Sam sat back in his chair and said: "That was the best meal I've had since I was home at Christmas."

"Thank you, Samuel," she said. "It's a great pleasure to have you home again. I hope you won't go gallivanting off now that you've finished college."

"Of course he won't," Jonas said. "He's going to work in the bank tomorrow morning."

Sam didn't argue. He'd said enough in the bank that afternoon. If he hadn't made it clear, he didn't know what he could say that would. He turned to his mother as he said: "Kitty left home this afternoon. She's in the hotel. I've asked her to marry me tomorrow, but she says no as long as trouble's in the air the way it is."

Jonas glared at Sam. He said: "I told you once today you are not marrying the Nickels girl. If you can't or won't obey my wishes, I ..."

"Don't say it, Jonas," his wife broke in.

"Don't say what?" Sam asked.

"I think I'd better say it," Jonas snapped. "Samuel, I expect to be obeyed by my son. I told your mother a while ago that if you don't obey me, you can't live here and I will disinherit you."

Mrs. Cassidy rose, her face pale. "Jonas, I have done exactly what you wanted me to as completely as I could from the day we were married, but if you do what you just said, I'll leave you."

She started to cry, then she fled into the bedroom and slammed the door behind her. Jonas looked at Sam as if he were the injured one. "Now why is she taking on like that?"

Sam studied his father for a moment and decided he really didn't know. He said: "If you can't answer that question, I can't tell you." He left the table.

VI

Pete Nickels was two years younger than Kitty and four years younger than the twins, so right from the time he could walk he'd had the short end of the stick. It wasn't so much the difference in age that mattered as it was the difference in disposition and build. Like Kitty, he had inherited his father's coloring and dark eyes and black hair, and that was all.

Pete didn't enjoy fighting; he lacked the hard-muscled strength of his brothers. He was tall and slender and long-boned. He read everything he could get his hands on and he had, with Kitty's help, persuaded Black Mike that he should have an education, so he had been allowed to stay in town with Kitty and finish high school. In the fall he would start college in Laramie, but between now and then he would herd sheep.

He knew that it was the best bargain he could wangle from his hard-headed father, but he wasn't sure he could get through the three summer months. He hated sheep. To him they were snot-nosed, stupid animals that insisted on doing the wrong thing if you'd let them, but he never told his father or the twins how he felt. That would have been as foolish as to tell them he loved poetry, which, as a matter of fact, he did.

Now, a few hours before Black Mike had said he was going to

cross the deadline, Pete was in charge of the entire Nickels band and he was scared. He'd been scared from the time Black Mike had told him that he was taking the twins into Cañon to buy ammunition and supplies, but he didn't tell his father or brothers about that, either. He doubted that they had ever been afraid of anything, but then at times he'd thought they weren't very bright.

Apparently it had never occurred to his father that Monk Corley and the cowmen might attack the sheep camp before the deadline was crossed, but it had occurred to Pete. He told himself that if he were Corley and he knew what the sheepmen planned to do, he'd hit hard before it was time for the showdown just to let his enemies know what they were up against.

Pete kept his Winchester in his hands all day. Now that it was dark, he stayed outside the wagon, leaving a lit lantern hanging inside. After the sheep were bedded down, he prowled around them through the aspens, stopping often to listen. The night would be a long one. He couldn't risk going to bed. Black Mike and the twins would be here early in the morning. After that, it would be their responsibility to protect the sheep, but tonight it was his.

He stopped in the aspens about fifty feet from the wagon. He had heard the cry of a coyote from some rim to the north and he sensed the loneliness of that cry. He was lonely, too, growing up in a family that had little understanding of him, growing up in the shadow of two older and bigger brothers who could always take out their frustrations on him.

He looked up into the cloudless sky. There was no moon, but the stars seemed brighter than they had ever been before; the air was more strongly scented with pine and sage smell than he could remember. He felt a prickle run down his spine, a strange feeling coming to him that this was the last night, a night when all the sensations of life were felt more keenly than on any other night.

Then, suddenly, his thoughts were jerked back to the reality of this moment when he heard a horse coming upgrade through the timber. He faded farther back into the aspens, listening to the horse as it moved closer. His muscles were tense, his nerves taut, his finger tight on the trigger until he realized what he was doing. He relaxed, his thumb moving to the hammer.

He couldn't figure this. If the cowmen were expecting to hit the sheep camp tonight, they wouldn't send one man to do the job. But it wasn't Black Mike or one of the twins because Black Mike was an inflexible man who made his plans and then followed them to the letter. He had told Pete he'd be back in the morning with the twins, and Pete was convinced there was no power short of hell or high water that would change his mind.

The horse came on steadily, the rider obviously knowing where he was heading. He reached the wagon and reined up in the finger of lantern light that fell through the open door. It was Kitty.

"Pete," the girl called, "are you in there?"

He ran toward her, breathing hard, shocked by surprise because she was the last person he expected to see. When he found his voice, he called hoarsely: "Kitty! I'm over here. Get out of the light."

She reined around and rode toward him, asking: "What are you doing out here?"

He reached her horse, still breathing hard, and held up a hand to help her down. As she dismounted, he said: "I'm trying to stay alive. That's why I'm here. I figure we'll have callers before morning. When I heard you coming, I thought it was one of them."

She put her hands on his arms and stared at him in the starlight. He tried to see her face, but it was a dark oval without expression. He knew, though, that she was worried or she wouldn't have ridden out here after dark.

"Has anything happened that makes you think that?" she asked finally.

"No. I'm just jumpy, I guess. It makes sense, though. Everybody knows Pa's making his move in the morning. It stands to reason that Corley and some of his friends will hit us tonight, figuring that's the way to show Pa they mean business."

"Sam Cassidy's home," Kitty said. "He's going to be Faraday's deputy. He came to see me, and Pa told the twins to throw him off the place. Instead of that happening, he knocked them both out, then Pa told me I wasn't to see Sam, so I left home and moved into the hotel."

"Good." Pete laughed softly, remembering the times the twins had slapped him around. He still wasn't big enough or strong enough to fight either of them effectively. "I wish I could have seen it."

"I didn't see the fight," Kitty said. "I was out back and didn't know Sam was there until he laid them out on the grass. It was kind of funny, seeing them peaceful that way for a little while, but I guess Pa didn't see it that way."

"I'll bet he didn't."

"What I started to say was that Sam doesn't think there'll be trouble before morning. I didn't think so, either, but something might happen just about daylight before Pa and the boys get here. I don't see any reason for you to stay and get beaten or killed because Pa is a bull-headed man who has created a situation that's bound to get somebody killed."

"I don't see any reason for it, either," Pete said, "but I am here and I'm alone. Or I was till you got here. Now you ride back to town before something does happen. I don't want you hurt no matter what happens to me."

She gripped his shoulders. "Now you listen to me, Pete. We're different from the twins and Pa. We're more like Ma was, I guess. Anyhow, Pa drove me out of the house. I'm going to marry Sam. You can live with us. That's why I rode out here. I got to thinking about it after Sam left me in the hotel. You know, the way we've been raised and all. We don't owe Pa anything. Not after what he's done."

"I'd like to live with you and Sam," Pete said as if he were arguing with a child, "but it's like I said. I'm looking after the sheep. I'm stuck here till morning."

"You can saddle your horse and ride out of here," Kitty said hotly. "You don't have to stay."

"I can't ride out and you know it. I'm not much of a man the way Pa sees it. Or the way Rory and Shawn look at things, but I am man enough to stay on the job and not duck out because I'm scared."

"Oh, Pete, you don't have to ..." She stopped, then whispered: "Somebody's coming."

He'd heard them, too. More than one horse this time, three or maybe four, coming upgrade and following just about the same course Kitty had taken. Pete said: "You get farther back in the quaking aspens. No matter what happens, you stay there. Don't make a sound."

"You stay here, too," she said. "You can't fight four or five of them."

But he was gone, moving silently through the white trunks of the aspens. A short time later he saw three men ride around the wagon and rein up in front of the door. They wore flour sacks over their faces, eye holes the only openings.

One was a big man who bellowed: "Nickels, come on out!" The man next to him was middle size and might have been anyone, but the third man was so tiny he was almost a midget. He was Scotty Doane, Pete thought, the only cowman in the country who was that small. It could have been a ten- or twelve-year-old boy, but he was certain they wouldn't bring a boy to help do a dirty job like this, and he didn't doubt that it was a dirty job.

For a moment Pete stood motionlessly, then he decided they wouldn't kill him. Probably they'd try to knock him out or tie him up or something just to keep him quiet while they slaughtered the sheep. That, of course, was something he would not allow.

He was reasonably sure the big man was Monk Corley, judging from his size and his voice. Pete moved forward, the hammer of his rifle back. He called: "Don't start anything because I've got a rifle and I'm holding it on you, Corley! What do you want?"

The big man didn't say a word. He must have been holding

his .45 in his hand because he fired the instant Pete asked what he wanted. The boy took the heavy slug in his chest, his finger automatically jerking the trigger, but the shot was wild. He felt himself falling and falling and falling into a deep bottomless well, and then the blackness was all around him and he felt nothing.

VII

Kitty had to hold her hand over her mouth to hold back the screams. She couldn't believe this was really happening. It had to be a dream, a horrible, spine-chilling nightmare, and yet in the back of her mind she knew this was the very thing she had been afraid might happen.

She heard the small man cry out, and then say angrily: "Damn it, Monk, you said there wouldn't be no killing."

"You heard him," the big man snapped. "He recognized me. You think I was going to let him run to Faraday and tell him who it was that killed the damned sheep? Fire the wagon, Scotty. I'll drag his carcass back a piece so it won't burn."

The big man was Monk Corley, the little one Scotty Doane, but she had no guess at all about the middle one. She watched Corley dismount and stoop and grab Pete by the feet and drag him deeper into the aspens. Corley was moving toward her. Her heart pounded violently, but she froze where she was, afraid to move. If they discovered her, they would kill her just as they had killed Pete because Corley could not risk leaving a witness to his crime. Then he dropped Pete's feet and wheeled and strode to his horse, and she was able to breathe again. If she hadn't retreated back into the quaking aspens as Pete had told her, Corley would have seen her.

Doane had gone into the wagon. He must have found the

coal-oil can and splashed it around the bottom of the wagon. It blazed up brightly like a great torch in a matter of seconds. Both Corley and Doane mounted and with the third man rode toward the sheep. She would have been dead now if Corley had come a few more feet toward her. There was enough light from the burning wagon for him to have seen her if he hadn't turned back at the time he did.

She didn't doubt Pete was dead, but she had to know for sure. She ran to his body and kneeled beside him. No pulse at all. She saw the dark stain on his shirt. She touched it and felt his warm blood. He must have died almost the instant he was shot.

For a time she didn't move. She told herself she didn't care if they came back and killed her. After her mother had died, Pete was the only one of her family she loved. She had never understood her father or the twins. In a way she hated them. At least she hated their fighting and drinking, and she hated sheep. She hated living on the ranch, and it had not been until Black Mike had bought the town house and she and Pete had moved into it for most of the year that she had felt she was a human being.

Now it seemed to her that her father was really the one who had murdered Pete. If he had lived, Pete would have gone to college. He might have become a great writer. Maybe a poet. A lawyer like Sam was going to be. Or a teacher. But no, he was dead at the age of eighteen, dead because of a sense of duty that had kept him here with the sheep.

Why couldn't Black Mike have ordered Rory or Shawn, or both of them, to stay here and guard the sheep? If somebody had to die, it had better have been one of the twins because neither one was ever going to be any different than he was right now.

She heard the shooting and knew they were killing the sheep. She couldn't stay here. She had to see Sam. Maybe he would be too late, but she had to get him. He might be able to track the killers, or maybe her identification would be enough.

She slipped back through the aspens to her horse, stepped into the saddle, and rode downgrade toward Cañon. Then her self-control broke and she began to cry. She gripped the horn, and swayed back and forth in the saddle, the tears running down her face. She still thought she heard gunfire long after she knew the sound could not possibly carry that far.

Maybe it was something she would hear all of her life. She had not believed Corley would actually do this, at least not until the deadline had been crossed. To slaughter sheep mercilessly and uselessly was bad enough, but to murder an eighteen-year-old boy was so bad it was unthinkable. She found it impossible to comprehend how any man could be capable of committing such a brutal crime; it was a kind of evil that had no logical explanation unless the murderer was a maniac, and Corley wasn't. She knew as well as she knew anything that the people of Cañon would not believe he had done it.

Kitty reached Cañon before the first hint of dawn showed anywhere in the eastern sky. She went directly to the Cassidy house, wanting nothing to do with her father or the twins. She dismounted wearily, staggering a little when her feet touched the ground. As she walked up the path to the front door, she told herself she didn't know what she would do if Jonas Cassidy came to the door. He had no more affection for her than Black Mike had for Sam, and she certainly had no real respect for him.

At least Black Mike was a strong man who was a fighter for what he believed was right, but Jonas was a toady. He would fawn all over Monk Corley to keep his favor. He was the same with the other cattlemen because in that way he let everyone know which side he was on, with the result that the cowmen kept their money in his bank. She had never known him to stand up and fight for a principle unless it meant dollars and cents profit for him.

She yanked the bell pull three times before she heard anyone, then a light appeared in the hall and the door opened. Jonas Cassidy stood there, the lamp held high in his hand, the robe that was tied around his waist covering only about half of his spindly legs.

"I want to see Sam," Kitty said.

He peered at her, apparently not recognizing her until that moment. He scowled, sour-tempered because he had been awakened from a sound sleep. He said irritably: "You're a fool for coming here at this time of night to see Sam. I told him at supper he was not marrying you, so you might as well go away."

It was too much, Pete's being murdered by men Jonas Cassidy claimed as friends. She wanted to slap him, simply to push him out of her way as she would a bug or a useless dog that was without teeth. He started to close the door. She could not allow that. Trembling and surprised at her own audacity, she jammed her booted right foot forward and blocked the door.

"You call Sam or I'll go upstairs to his room," she said. "I'm not here because I'm going to marry him. I'm here because he's deputy sheriff. I've just seen my brother Pete murdered."

He blinked, then shook his head. "I suspect you are a very excitable young lady. In the first place I don't believe your brother has been murdered. In the second place, Sam will be working in the bank, not as Ben Faraday's deputy. Oh, I know that's what he says, but give him a little time and he'll see that his bread is buttered on the side I ..."

No use to argue with this cheap little imitation of a man. She pushed him into the hall, forcing him to back up, spluttering something about her trespassing, then she began to scream: "Sam! Sam!"

Jonas tried to shush her, but she kept on screaming.

VIII

Sam was sound asleep when he was partially awakened by the commotion downstairs. He turned over, thinking sleepily that he had been dreaming, then he heard a woman scream: "Sam! Sam!" He hit the floor and pulled on his pants, having the crazy idea that it was Kitty who had yelled. He was still groggy from sleep when he ran down the stairs to find his father trying to push Kitty out through the front door and Kitty refusing to be pushed and continuing to scream: "Sam!"

"I'm here, Kitty," he said. "See? I'm here."

She was hysterical. It took a little time for her to realize he actually was there. When she did, she began to cry. Sam led her into the front room, his father trotting along behind him, holding the lamp and saying over and over: "I don't want her in the house. I don't want her in the house."

Sam eased Kitty into a rocking chair as his mother came out of the bedroom wearing a robe, her hair down her back. She took the lamp from Jonas as she said: "I don't care whether you want her in the house or not. She's here. Now shut up."

Jonas stared at his wife as if he could not believe she had really said it. He chewed his lower lip, silent, suddenly becoming a helpless little man who was not even obeyed in his own home. Mrs. Cassidy kneeled on one side of Kitty and Sam on the other.

"I'll build a fire and fix some tea," Mrs. Cassidy said.

"No, I'm all right." Kitty swallowed and turned her head to look at Sam. "They murdered Pete tonight. There were three of them. I went out there to get him to leave the sheep camp. I didn't think anything would happen tonight, but I was afraid it would happen early in the morning before Pa and the boys got there. I was wrong. They didn't wait till morning. They would have killed me, too, if they'd seen me."

Sam sat there frozen, looking at the girl and thinking that this must be a nightmare. He'd had nightmares so real that he was sure they were happening, then he'd wake up and find that it wasn't really happening and he would lie back in bed, a cold sweat covering his body. Then he knew he wasn't going to wake up and find that this was a nightmare; it was real, the most horrible thing he had ever heard about in his whole life. Pete, the only one of the Nickels boys he had liked.

His mother asked: "Do you know who the men were?"

"The one who fired the shot was Monk Corley," Kitty answered. "One of the others was Scotty Doane. I don't know who the third one was."

"How do you know it was Corley?" Sam asked. "Were you close enough to see their faces?"

"They wore flour sacks or something like that over their faces," Kitty said, "but I heard Doane call the big man Monk. Besides, I recognized his voice and I couldn't mistake his build."

"Corley wouldn't do a thing like that," Jonas said hoarsely. "I know him too well. Not unless it was a fight, and even then he wouldn't do it until your sheep were across the deadline."

No one looked at him or argued with him. It was as if he wasn't even there. Sam said: "Tell us what happened. All of it."

She did, starting with her thoughts and fears as she'd argued them with herself in the hotel room after Sam had left her. When she was finished, she said: "I came to you, Sam, because you said you were Ben Faraday's deputy. I didn't think Ben was well enough to do anything. When I got here, your father wouldn't let me see you."

Again Sam ignored his father, even when Jonas said: "You won't arrest Monk, Samuel. If it happened the way this girl says it did, some other man about Monk's size did the shooting. I tell you it wasn't Monk. I talked to him about it this afternoon and he assured me he wouldn't make a move unless the sheep were driven across the deadline."

Sam rose. "I'll get my clothes on and take your horse to the livery stable, then I'll tell Ben about it and see what he wants me to do. They won't be there by the time I get to the sheep camp and there's not much chance we can pick up any tracks that will help."

Mrs. Cassidy said: "Come into the kitchen, Kitty. You didn't have any supper last night, did you?"

"No, I wasn't hungry."

"I'll build a fire and fix something. I could stand a cup of coffee myself."

"I don't want any kin of Black Mike Nickels in my house," Jonas said peevishly.

Sam went to his room and Mrs. Cassidy led Kitty into the kitchen and closed the door. When Sam came downstairs, his gun belt was buckled around him. His Colt was in the holster, his Winchester in his right hand. Jonas was still standing in the middle of the front room. Seeing Sam, he ran into the hall, shouting: "If you try to arrest Monk, I won't be responsible for what happens! I think Black Mike sent the girl here to lie about this so you'd arrest Monk and …"

Sam didn't stop to listen to what his father had to say. He never heard the rest of the sentence, but his mind was made up on one thing. When he got back to town, he'd gather up his belongings and move into the hotel. Kitty was right about getting married now. The hotel would have to do until this trouble blew over and he and Kitty could settle down to normal married life. He had no idea how long it would take to blow over, but it was coming to a head in a hurry.

He left Kitty's horse in the livery stable, then strode to the courthouse, angled across one corner of the yard, and went on across the street to Ben Faraday's cabin. He knocked only once; Faraday must have been awake. He called: "Who is it?"

"Sam Cassidy."

"Come in." When Sam opened the door, and stepped inside, the sheriff said: "I had a hunch it was you, and I've got another hunch, too. It'd take a hell of a lot of trouble to fetch you here this time of night. Light the lamp on the table and let's hear it."

Sam leaned his Winchester against the wall. He struck a match and, lifting the chimney from the lamp, touched the flame to the wick, and then replaced the chimney. He drew up a chair and sat down beside the bunk. Faraday's thin face was covered by white stubble, and, in the dim light from the lamp, he looked even more fragile than he had during the afternoon when Sam had talked to him.

Faraday didn't move or say a word as Sam told him what had happened. When he finished, Faraday said: "Well, you didn't get home a day too soon. I'm like your dad in one way, though. I can't believe Monk would be stupid enough to do this before the sheep crossed the deadline. He's reasonably smart, Sam. He'd know that public opinion wouldn't stand still for murder in this county. Twenty years ago, yes, but not now."

"Looking at it from Corley's standpoint, this isn't so stupid," Sam said. "He'd want to hit hard and hit first to stop Black Mike before he got started. This way he probably hoped to keep Dale Sontag out of the county. For another thing, he couldn't guess that Kitty would see the whole thing. He probably had told Scotty Doane there wouldn't be a murder. Chances are he never intended to kill Pete. If Pete hadn't mentioned his name, I doubt that he would have shot him."

"Yeah," Faraday admitted, "you're saying it purty well. Now I'll go one more. Kitty's testimony won't carry much weight, her being Black Mike's daughter and Pete's sister. She didn't see Monk's face, so the defense can claim it might be a complete stranger like the men who tried to stop you on the pass."

"Corley would still be involved if that was true," Sam said.

"Being involved, if you can prove it, still ain't murder," Faraday said. "No, it'll take better evidence than her testimony to put a rope on Monk's neck."

"I'll get a statement out of Scotty Doane," Sam said. "He's not very skookum when it comes to things like this."

"The defense will say he made the statement under pressure," Faraday said. "Scotty will get up on the witness stand and say it was a lie." He sat up and began to dress, and then he added in a tone of futility: "Sam, you're figuring on reading law. Well, you'd best have a talk with Judge Murray. He'll tell you some of the facts of life. It don't make much difference how honest you are or how much you want to see justice done. Convicting a cowman in this country for a crime against a sheepman is a tough proposition."

"But this is murder," Sam said. "Just a minute ago you told me this county wouldn't stand for it today, even though it would have twenty years ago."

Faraday nodded as he tugged on his boots. "I know what I said. If we had good, solid evidence to back up Kitty's story, we'd have Monk dead to rights. We'd get a conviction for murder, though maybe not for shooting sheep. You go ahead and get your statement from Scotty Doane, but it's not the kind of evidence we need."

He picked up his gun belt and buckled it around him, then took his Winchester off the antler rack by the door. "Let's saddle up. I've got a roan in the shed you can ride. He's a better animal than you'll get from the stable."

"I can ride out there alone if you don't feel ..." Sam began.

"Sure you can," Faraday said, "but I guess I can ride that far this morning. Come on."

They went out into the pale morning light, Sam knowing it would be foolish to try to talk Faraday out of going. He was a man who would rather die in the saddle than in bed, and for him, Sam told himself, it would be the best way.

IX

The sun was showing above the eastern horizon by the time Faraday and Sam reached the first of the scattered aspens. The riding was hurting Faraday. Sam saw it in the older man's face, but he didn't urge the sheriff to turn back. He knew there was no use. Also, he wanted Faraday along if they ran into Black Mike and the twins.

Presently they passed the Augie Pope cabin. Faraday jerked a thumb toward it. "That's Doc Harvey's rig yonder. Augie came to town late yesterday afternoon and asked Doc to come out. You know Augie and his missus were married close to twenty years before she got pregnant. Doc said she'd have a hard time with the baby, having narrow hips like she's got, so he figured he'd be here a long time. Looks like he figured right."

Sam remembered Augie Pope, a rancher about like Scotty Doane who'd owned a ten-cow spread here in the foothills of the Bearpaws for years. There were dozens of little ranchers scattered through these hills just like Doane and Pope, men who squeezed a poor living from their ranches and probably wouldn't have survived this long if they hadn't made a habit of eating deer, antelope, and Monk Corley's beef.

Corley knew he lost a good many steers every year in this way, but he never made an issue out of it. It was a sort of unwritten law that they could eat his beef if they didn't take advantage of the privilege. In exchange, they supported him in any issue that came up in the Cattlemen's Association, and if he picked a man in a local election, he had their votes. The townsmen, the farmers, and Black Mike Nickels outnumbered the cowmen, but Sam had never known them to combine to beat a candidate that Corley backed. He thought about this as they rode, and he told himself he'd have a hard time getting elected sheriff if he did decide to run next November.

Then another thought occurred to him. Monk Corley and the other two men must have ridden right past Augie Pope's cabin last night and again this morning after they had slaughtered the sheep. This might not be the solid proof Faraday said they'd need, but if either the doctor or Pope saw Corley and his friends ride by, it would help to confirm Kitty's story. As they started up the switchbacks, Sam considered this carefully. Augie Pope wasn't very bright, and he might be trapped into admitting he had seen the three ranchers, but Doc Harvey was another proposition. He was like Jonas Cassidy and most of the townsmen, reluctant to say or do anything that would rub Corley the wrong way.

They stopped once to blow the horses. Faraday stepped down and studied the soft dirt of the road. It had rained the day before and the tracks were clear enough to an expert like Faraday. He rose and swung into the saddle, saying: "Looks like Kitty came up and went down just as she said. Three other riders done the same. We didn't much more than miss the three when they went down. Their tracks are purty fresh."

"Then they must have ridden past Augie's place after it was light," Sam said, "but they didn't go into town or we would have met them."

"They wouldn't do that," Faraday said. "They split up at the foot of the grade and went three different ways is my guess. They naturally wouldn't want to be seen together." He scratched his nose, frowning, and added: "I had the same notion about Doc or Augie seeing 'em, and if we had their testimony, it sure would help. How do you figure to get 'em to talk?"

"I doubt that Doc will, but Augie might," Sam said.

"It's worth stopping for when we go back down," Faraday said. "If Missus Pope had the baby, it might work, but if she hasn't, we'd better go on. Augie was sure excited when he got to town yesterday. He kept asking us whether God would take the baby now that it's gone this far? They're both over forty, you know, and gave up any idea of having a baby years ago."

"I hope they both make it, mother and baby," Sam said. "It's a good bet that Augie and Doc were both awake when Corley and his friends rode past."

"Sure they were," Faraday agreed. "Well, you're going to be hungry before you get back."

"I can stand it," Sam said. "How about you?"

Faraday grinned wryly. "I never get hungry no more. I eat 'cause I think I've got to, but it's a chore, forcing the grub down."

They went on, making the last steep climb through the aspens and coming out into the small park that had held the sheep camp. Here they found exactly what they had expected—Pete's body with the dark stain of dried blood on his shirt, the charred remains of the wagon, and a great many dead sheep. Sam didn't try to count them, but he guessed there were several hundred.

When he returned to Faraday who was carefully examining the ground around the wagon, he said: "They didn't kill the whole band. I guess they drove the rest away."

Faraday nodded absent-mindedly, his gaze on the ground. Finally he turned to Sam. "Kitty must have been scared. You said she was hysterical when you talked to her."

"That may have been because Dad was so ornery about her wanting to see me," Sam said.

"That would sure help," Faraday said. "I was thinking that what happened was enough to make an ordinary girl go crazy, but she gave you a straight account of what happened. I mean, the sign all bears out what she said, even to Corley dragging the body away from the burning wagon. He got damned close to her, too. If he'd gone about ten feet farther, he probably would have spotted her, even as dark as it was, and if he had, you wouldn't have no girl to marry."

Sam stared at Pete's body, the thin face hard set in death and bearing little resemblance to the boy Sam remembered. Suddenly he felt a wave of fury rush through him so violently that he would have killed Monk Corley if the big man had been there. He didn't for a minute doubt what Faraday had just said. Corley would have murdered Kitty if he had seen her.

Sam turned away, his fists knotted at his sides. Faraday said: "Pete's horse is yonder in that pole corral. Saddle him and we'll take the body back to town."

Sam didn't say anything for a moment. Black Mike Nickels and the twins had just come into sight. Finally he said: "Black Mike or one of the boys can do it."

Faraday nodded. "Sure, I didn't see them riding in." He laid a hand on Sam's arm. "Hang onto your temper, boy. This ain't gonna be easy."

"It sure as hell won't," Sam said. "I may wind up telling Mike he had a part in killing Pete."

"Don't do it," Faraday said. "I've never seen the day when you could tell Black Mike anything."

"This may be the day for me to try," Sam said.

The Nickels men were close enough to see what was left of the wagon and some of the dead sheep. Black Mike let out a bellowed oath and motioned wildly toward the slaughtered animals, apparently ordering the twins to take a closer look at them, then he came on toward Sam and Faraday at a hard run.

Black Mike reined up ten feet from Faraday and swung down, bawling: "What in the God damn' hell has gone on around here and what are you doing here?"

Faraday stepped aside and pointed to Pete's body. Apparently Black Mike hadn't seen it before. He had started toward Faraday, his great hands fisted as if he thought the sheriff had done this. He stopped, his mouth dropping open, his eyes bugging out of his head, and then dropped down immediately.

Sam and Faraday stood motionlessly, watching, not knowing what to expect. Sam decided that what happened was the last thing he could have expected. He had never seen Black Mike show any soft emotion. Anger and hate, but never grief or sorrow or regret for anything he had done. Now the big man cried. For what seemed a long time he hunkered beside the boy, his head tipped forward, his great body shaking with sobs. Finally he rose, tears still rolling down his cheeks. He took a bandanna out of his pocket and wiped his eyes, then he blew his nose.

"Corley done this, didn't he?" Nickels asked hoarsely.

"We have evidence that says he did," Faraday agreed. "Whether it'll stick in court is something else."

"I'll kill him," Black Mike said. "By God, I'll kill him. I ain't waiting for no cowman's court to turn him loose."

"Then I'll arrest you for murder," Faraday said, "and I'll tell you one thing I know for sure. In this county there will be no trouble convicting a sheepman for murdering a cowman."

Black Mike wiped a hand across his face, then he walked to what was left of the wagon and kicked around pots and pans, and finally turned back to Faraday. "What evidence have you got on Corley?"

"We have an eyewitness," Faraday said. "The problem is that Corley and two men with him wore flour sacks or something like that over their heads."

"Who saw 'em?"

"Kitty," Sam answered.

"Kitty?" Black Mike repeated the name as if he didn't know who she was. "You mean my daughter? She wouldn't be up here ..."

He wiped a big hand across his face again, then he blurted: "What was she doing here?"

"You'll have to ask her," Sam said.

"You're damn' right I'll ask her!" he shouted. "And I'm gonna ask you if you're fixing to arrest Corley."

"I ain't sure," Faraday said. "Sam has got some idea. If we can get enough evidence ..."

"Evidence, hell. If Kitty seen the bastard ..." He stopped, his black eyes narrowing and growing hard. "Now you listen to me, you sanctimonious son-of-a-bitch. If you think you can keep Corley from swinging because he's a cattleman and you're a cattleman ..."

Sam stepped forward, the fury churning in him again. No one had any grounds for attacking Faraday's integrity on the ground that he was soft on cowmen because he was a cowman, and for a man like Black Mike to do it now, with Faraday as sick as he was, seemed too much.

"You shut up, Mike," Sam said. "Now you do a little listening. We think Monk Corley pulled the trigger, but you tell me who gave Pete the job of taking care of your sheep when the whole country was about to explode on account of you moving sheep across the deadline and with you threatening to bring in Dale Sontag?"

Black Mike glared at him. He said sullenly: "If you think I'm to blame for my boy's murder ..."

"That's exactly what I think," Sam said. "If Kitty hadn't been lucky, she'd have been killed, too. You didn't come up here last night to give Pete a hand. You didn't send Rory and Shawn out here to help him. I've got a notion to arrest you for criminal negligence." He saw the big man stiffen, his mouth set into a tight line as Sam's words hit home, before he added: "And for being an accessory before the fact. Come on, Ben. Let's ride."

Sam wheeled away. Faraday said: "He didn't really mean that, Mike, but I am asking you to stay out of this. I may call on you for help if we need it. Arresting Monk and keeping him in jail ain't gonna be easy."

Faraday followed Sam to the horses. They mounted and rode away, neither looking back. Black Mike stood motionlessly staring at them, and then began to cry again.

X

Both Doc Harvey and Augie Pope were hunkered down in front of Pope's cabin when Faraday and Sam reined up, Faraday calling: "How'd it go, Augie?"

Pope jumped up and started prancing around like an exuberant teenager. "I've got a boy, Ben. By God, I've got a boy, and me forty-four years old and married twenty years."

"Congratulations," Faraday said, smiling. "How's the missus?"

"She's doing fine," Doc Harvey said. "She was in labor a long time and she's awful tired now, but she's going to be all right."

"Well now," Faraday said, "I'm glad for both of you, Augie. When the missus is up and around, you bring her and the boy into town and I'll stand you to a dinner at the hotel."

"That's right kind of you," Pope said. "We'll sure take you up on it."

"Good," Faraday said. "I'll be looking forward to it. It's folks like you and your missus that makes this the best county in Wyoming. Oh, say, did either of you happen to notice anybody riding by here last night?"

"Yes, we did," Doc Harvey said quickly. "I was outside here. I don't remember what time it was, but it wasn't midnight yet. We had a fire going and some water heating, and it was hotter'n the hinges of hell inside the house. I stepped outside to cool off and I heard this horsebacker going upgrade. It was dark, so I didn't have any idea who it was."

"Anybody ride by later on?" Faraday asked. "In the morning? About dawn, maybe?"

"I seen 'em," Pope said. "Just getting daylight and ..."

"Now hold on, Augie," Harvey said. "I was with you. Remember? The missus just couldn't seem to have that baby and we were keeping the fire up and the water hot. It was still dark. Augie kind of forgot, being excited like he is, but it was one rider. I figured it was the same one we heard going upgrade earlier in the night."

"But damn it," Pope spluttered, "we likewise seen ..."

"No, Augie," Harvey said. "You took too big a drink from that bottle when you saw you had a boy. Now I'm not saying that other riders didn't go past here last night, you understand. We were inside most of the time and a whole army could have ridden past without us knowing about it, but that's all we heard and we didn't see 'em either time, as dark as it was."

"Thanks," Faraday said. "If you recollect something else, Doc, let me know."

Faraday and Sam rode toward town, Augie Pope staring at the doctor as if he wasn't sure which one had lost his memory. When they were fifty yards down the road, Sam said: "They saw Corley and the other two ride past this morning and it was light enough to recognize them, but Doc Harvey figured it was best to keep mum. It was like you thought, Ben, only I'm wondering if Doc will go on keeping his mouth shut after he knows it was murder."

"Hard to tell," Faraday said. "I think I'll ride back up here in a day or two and see if I can get anything out of Augie."

"I don't think you will," Sam said. "Not after Doc explains a few things to him. In the long run it'll be Doc who talks if he decides he ought to. He's his own man and Augie's not."

"Yeah, I guess you're right," Faraday said. "I dunno that Augie's word would count much, but Doc's would. Everybody respects him. He might even swing your dad over."

Sam laughed shortly. "That would be quite a trick, Ben."

When they reached town, Faraday stepped down in front of his cabin, then stood beside his horse for a moment, one hand holding the saddle horn. He said: "Put 'em up, will you, Sam? I'm going to bed."

"I'll take care of them," Sam said, and wondered if Faraday would still be here for Monk Corley's trial.

Sam rode around the cabin to the shed, leading Faraday's mount. He stripped gear from both animals, fed and watered them, and stepped into the cabin before he went home. Faraday was in bed, completely exhausted.

"I'm going home to eat dinner," Sam said, "then I'm coming back for the roan and I'll ride out to see Scotty Doane. Maybe it won't do any more good than you think, but if he does make a statement and names Corley, I'm going to arrest the bastard whether we've got enough to hang him or not."

For a time Faraday didn't say anything. His eyes were wide open and he was staring at the ceiling. Sam waited, knowing the sheriff had something on his mind and there was no way to hurry him.

"All right, you go ahead," Faraday said finally. "Just be sure you do it right so you get him without starting a civil war. I know what will happen when you try to arrest him. Every cowboy in town will jump in on Monk's side. It'll be a hell of a job even if I'm on my feet and helping you."

"You were thinking of something else besides that," Sam said. "You knew that I knew everything you just said."

Faraday turned his head on the pillow enough to look at Sam. He said: "That's right, I was, but I don't know the answer to what I was thinking. The question is whether this is the time. We'll have Kitty's testimony and we'll have this statement you're gonna get out of Doane, only it'll be thrown out of court. What I don't know is whether it would be smarter to wait to see if Monk makes a mistake. He ain't gonna run. You know that."

Sam nodded. "I've thought the same you're thinking. My hunch is that he's more likely to make a mistake if we have him in jail."

"I don't know," Faraday said dully. "You go ahead and do what you think you have to. You're the one who'll be taking the chances."

"Looks like we've got to take it one step at a time," Sam said. "The first step is to go after Scotty Doane. I'll tell you how I make out."

"Good luck," Faraday said.

Sam walked home, thinking that Faraday had reached the place where he didn't care much either way—he was that sick and that weak. The Ben Faraday who lay flat on his back in bed bore little resemblance to the Ben Faraday for whom Sam had worked the previous summer. It was nearly noon when Sam reached his home. He found his mother and Kitty in the kitchen. Mrs. Cassidy was hovering over the stove, her face dark with anger. Kitty sat at the table, her eyes red. Sam dropped into a chair beside her and took her hands.

"How do you feel?" he asked.

"Pretty awful," she said. "I keep seeing Pete there in the darkness when I was talking to him and those men riding up and Corley shooting him and dragging his body away from the wagon. It's kind of like watching shadows in front of you. They won't go away, but you can't reach out and touch them, either."

"It's going to take time," he said. "A lot of time." He told her about talking to her father, and added: "He'll want to see you, I suppose, but don't let him upset you. He's just about as much to blame for Pete's death as Corley is. I aim to keep telling him that until he gets it through that thick skull of his."

"I've been wondering if I was to blame," she said miserably. "I think I should have gone with Pete when he went back to the wagon and stood up to Corley. If I'd've done that, maybe he wouldn't have shot either one of us."

"You don't know Monk Corley," Sam said. "He'd have killed both of you, so quit blaming yourself right now."

"Or I could have shot him if I'd taken my gun," she said. "I thought the same thing Pete must have thought, that they'd come to kill sheep, not people."

"It's what anyone would have thought," Sam agreed.

"Dinner's ready," Mrs. Cassidy said as she brought a plate of hot biscuits to the table.

Sam pulled up his chair, and bowed his head as his mother said grace, then he glanced at her, not knowing whether he should ask the question that was in his mind or not. His mother looked directly at him, saying: "I'll tell you before you ask. Your father is not coming home for dinner. He's eating at the hotel."

That, of course, raised another question, but again Sam was reluctant to ask it. He had thought for years that his mother put up with far more than she should, but he sensed that she had finally reached the end of her string. Still, he hated to ask.

"I'm to blame," Kitty said miserably. "Your father wants me out of the house, but your mother asked me to stay."

"It's a very simple thing," Mrs. Cassidy said. "I love Sam. Sam loves you. I would be a poor kind of mother if I didn't love you, too, so I do want you to stay."

"But if Mister Cassidy ..." Kitty began.

"Mister Cassidy is made from the same mass of hard-headed stupidity that Mister Nickels is," Mrs. Cassidy said. "I've had enough of both of them." She nodded at Sam. "It's my opinion you should marry Kitty right away, but whether you do or not, I think I am leaving your father. It will depend on what he says when he comes home tonight."

Sam looked at his mother, smiling. "I used to think you would be perfect if you had a little more spirit. Now you are perfect."

"Thank you, Samuel," she said gravely, "but after all these years it isn't easy. It isn't easy at all."

XI

Scotty Doane's spread, the Box D, lay five miles west of Cañon. Monk Corley's MC and the other big spreads lay north and south of town on the same bench that held Cañon. The good grass was on this bench, or in the foothills between it and the Bearpaws, but out here it was desert with much sagebrush and little grass.

As Sam rode out of town, he wondered about men like Scotty Doane who faced a future that held no promise for anything better. Doane was a bachelor. His neighbors on the edge of the bench and on out into the desert were married men with families. Married or single, they barely existed. When Monk Corley and Rance Temple and the other big ranchers drove their pool herd to the railroad at Rawlins in the fall, the small fry threw their shirt-tail steers in with the others and received a few dollars that paid for the ammunition, clothes, and staples they had to have.

At best it was a poor life. All of them owed Doc Harvey, and most of them had a bill at Abe Kahn's Mercantile that was never quite paid. The children had little or no schooling. The women were old before they were thirty. The men weren't lazy, but all the hard work in the world wasn't enough in this arid land where drinking water often had to be hauled from town. Sam wondered as he did every time he rode out here why people stayed. Once he had asked Scotty Doane. Doane had been insulted. He had thrown his shoulders back and pushed out his flat chest and said: "I'm independent. That's what's worth staying for. If I moved to Rawlins or Rock Springs, I'd have to go to work for the railroad or in a coal mine, and I wouldn't even own my own soul."

He was independent, all right, Sam thought. At least he had the right to starve, but he wasn't independent in one sense and in that sense he didn't own his soul because he obeyed every order that came out of Monk Corley, even to murdering Pete Nickels and slaughtering the Nickels' sheep.

Doane knew as well as he knew anything that the moment he bucked Corley, he wouldn't be allowed to throw his cattle in with the others for the big fall drive and he'd lose the few cash dollars he made every year. It was the same with Augie Pope and the rest, and in effect Corley held them in a sort of economic servitude that meant they weren't independent at all. The more Sam thought about this and the closer he got to the Box D, the less certain he was that he'd get a statement out of Doane who would think first of all of how Corley had him boxed in between a rock and a blind cañon.

Sam rode up out of a deep gully, the Box D buildings directly in front of him, if they could be called buildings. There was a dirt-roofed and weather-beaten cabin, a pole corral, and a slab shed. That was all, and even so Doane somehow contrived to give an overall impression of trash. He was a collector of tin cans, parts of rusty machinery, broken-down wagons, and junk that was nameless, all scattered haphazardly around the place.

If Doane was awake and worried about being arrested, he might shoot first and ask questions later, Sam knew, and here he was a target as big as life. The thought had no more than gone through his mind than a rifle cracked from his cabin, the bullet snapping past uncomfortably close to Sam's head. This was the first time in Sam's life he had ever been shot at, and the feeling it gave him was not one that came from the pursuit of happiness. He spilled out of his saddle and scrambled over the lip of the gully as the rifle cracked again, the bullet kicking up dust a foot or so from his head before he went over the edge of the gully.

He rolled down the steep bank, stirring up a cloud of dust that almost choked him before he regained his feet and staggered along the bottom of the gully until he was clear of the dust and could take a good breath. He discovered he had lost his hat and went back to get it. Then he remembered his Winchester was in the boot; all he had was a revolver. He had to get closer to the cabin to do any good with it, and getting closer was a problem.

The shed might be the answer. Doane would be watching the place where he'd gone over the edge. At least Sam hoped he would. That would give him a chance to reach the shed before Doane spotted him. He ran along the gully that twisted back and forth aimlessly until he reached a place that he thought would put him in line with the shed. Sam knew he couldn't risk poking his head up to look. He had to come up out of the gully and run, and hope that Doane wouldn't see him soon enough to catch him in his sights. Doane used to be a good marksman. Sam remembered that from the turkey shoots they'd had in Cañon at Thanksgiving when Sam had been in high school. He doubted that a few years had changed Doane's skill for the worse. He might have improved. Maybe his near misses with those first two shots were exactly what he intended.

Sam didn't take time to think about it. The sooner he moved the better. He lunged over the edge of the ravine and started running, bending low and zigzagging. He hadn't gone quite far enough in the gully to be behind the shed. Doane had time for one good shot before Sam succeeded in getting the shed between him and the cabin. Again the shot was a near miss, the slug kicking up dust at Sam's feet, and then the shed was directly in front of him and he dived headlong toward it and lay flat on his belly, panting hard.

"Don't you come no closer!" Doane yelled. "I could have killed you with any one of those shots. Now you get on your horse and vamoose. I won't shoot again if I can see you're leaving."

Sam could stay here until dark, and then work his way to the cabin, but he had no intention of doing anything of the sort. Still, to leave the protection of the shed and rush the cabin would be instant suicide. Doane wouldn't let him get ten feet from the shed. That left one alternative, to talk Doane into surrendering.

"Scotty, you're under arrest for the murder of Pete Nickels!" Sam shouted. "Don't make it worse by resisting arrest."

"How can I make it worse?" Doane demanded. "You only hang a man once. I don't see how it could be any worse than it is."

"You didn't fire the shot," Sam said. "Monk Corley did. You wouldn't have gone with him if you'd known it would end up in murder. You told Corley that, but he said Pete recognized him and so he had to kill the boy."

Doane didn't say anything for a while and Sam grinned, thinking he must be shocked to find out that Sam knew this. Finally Doane asked, his voice shaky: "How'd you know that?"

"There was an eyewitness to the shooting," Sam said. "This witness will testify in court that you did not pull the trigger of the gun that murdered Pete."

Again Doane was silent for a minute or more, then he yelled: "You're hoorawing me! It was darker'n the inside of a black bull. There wasn't nobody else there. They couldn't have seen nothing if they had been there."

Sam considered this, not wanting to identify Kitty, but knowing it would come out sooner or later. It probably didn't make any difference whether he identified her now or next week. He'd better tell Doane. The man might crack if he knew exactly what had happened.

"The witness is Pete's sister Kitty," Sam said. "They were back in the trees talking when the three of you rode up. She stayed there. That's why none of you saw her. There was a lantern inside the wagon. You were in the light."

For the third time Doane was silent. Sam didn't know what was going to happen, but he was surprised when Doane said: "I'm coming out with my hands up, if you promise you won't shoot."

"I won't shoot you," Sam said, and wondered if this was a trap.

Trap or not, Scotty Doane came out of the cabin, his hands over his head. He wasn't wearing a gun in his holster. It struck Sam that this was too easy. Maybe Corley or the third man was in the cabin, and Sam would be smoked down the moment he showed himself. He remained at the corner of the shed, his revolver in his hand, watching as Doane crossed the yard to him.

Sam didn't stand up and move away from the shed until Doane stopped about five feet from him. He decided that no one else was in the cabin. He remembered Ben Faraday saying the three men would separate and go to their homes when they reached the foot of the grade. In any case, Sam knew it would be a mistake to let Doane sense he was afraid.

"I could have held you off till dark," Doane said, "and got clear, but if the girl seen all of this, and I figure she did or you wouldn't be telling me what happened, I'm better off in jail than I am running and hiding with you on my tail. Like you said, I'd just make it worse by resisting arrest."

"That's right." Sam holstered his .45 and, stepping up to the little man, ran his hands over him to check for a hide-out gun. "It looks to me like Corley will hang, but there's one thing you can do to help your situation. I want you to write out a statement telling what happened."

"Oh, no," Doane said. "Monk would have my hide if I done that. I'll go to jail and I'll sit there till I rot, but I ain't telling you nothing."

Sam stepped back and put his right hand on the butt of his gun, his lips curling in distaste. He said: "Put your hands down, Scotty, and then you listen to me." Doane lowered his hands, his wizened face showing his fear. "I'm here. Corley isn't. Now you think first of a couple of facts. First, Kitty is my girl. I love her and I'm going to marry her. I know Corley would have killed her if he had seen her last night. That right?"

Doane nodded. "I reckon he would have."

"Second fact. I don't like Black Mike or the twins much, but I did like Pete. He was just a boy. Murdering him was as low-down ornery mean as Monk Corley could get."

"I ain't arguing with you about that," Doane mumbled. "It wasn't my idea to kill him. I wouldn't have gone if I'd knowed that."

"It's going to take more than Kitty's word to hang Corley," Sam said. "Your statement will help and I aim to get it. Do you know what I'll do to you if you don't give it to me?"

Doane backed up and stared at Sam's face. What he saw did not reassure him. He said faintly: "I ain't sure."

"I thought you could guess." Sam drew his revolver. "I'll kill you, Scotty. I'll carry you back into your cabin and put your rifle in your hands and I'll fetch Ben Faraday out here to see how it was. He'll believe me when I tell him you were shot in a gunfight, resisting arrest. Now, maybe Corley will have your hide for making a statement. Just maybe. But there's one thing you can be sure of. I'll have your hide right now if you don't."

Doane began to tremble. He watched Sam bring his gun up, watched him thumb back the hammer, and then he broke. "All right. All right. I'll write any damned thing you say."

"Just the truth," Sam said. "We'll go into the cabin and put it down right now."

Doane turned and walked back to the cabin, Sam a step behind him. Sam didn't feel completely safe until he stepped inside and, looking around, saw that no one else was there. The mess and stink in the cabin was so bad he wondered how Doane could stand it. He watched the little man hunt for a pencil and some wrapping paper, and when he found them, he sat down at the table and wrote laboriously for a few minutes, then signed his name and brought the paper to Sam.

Monk Corley and Rance Temple and me went to the sheep camp to shoot sheep. Corley shot and kilt Pete. Me and Rance didn't know he was going to. We are inosent.

Scotty Doane

Sam nodded and, folding the paper, put it into his pocket. It was probably the best he could do. Doane might deny he had written it, or swear he had done so under duress, and the judge might throw it out of court. But it was another short step. At least it told Sam who the third man was.

"All right, Scotty," Sam said. "Saddle up. We're going to jail."

XII

Ben Faraday had not returned to his office in the courthouse when Sam locked Scotty Doane in a cell. Sam didn't wait to see the sheriff. Arresting Rance Temple was the next step and there was no point in waiting. On the other hand, time was of the essence. The man would be easier to take now than he would after he heard about Doane.

Rance Temple's Rafter T was only one mile north of town. It was a fine outfit, one of the best in the county, with hay meadows along the North Prong, winter pasture on the bench, and ample summer range in the high country of the Bearpaws. His wife had died the year before, and now he lived on the Rafter T with a housekeeper and ran the spread with the help of his five sons.

Sam rode into the Rafter T yard, not having any plan to take Temple. If the man's sons were home and elected to fight, Sam knew he would have trouble with the Rafter T, but it was still the middle of the afternoon and he had every right to think the boys would be out on the range at this time of day. Temple was sitting in the shade of the barn, working on some harness when Sam reined up. The youngest boy, fourteen-year-old Bud, was cleaning out a corral. Neither Temple nor the boy acted as if he saw Sam. Temple kept on fussing with the harness; the boy continued pitching forkfuls of manure into a wheelbarrow.

For what must have been a full minute Sam sat his saddle looking down at the rancher. Temple had always been, as far as Sam knew, a very solid citizen. He worked hard, he was law-abiding, he was a member of the school board, and he was not a man to gossip or slander his neighbor.

"How'd you ever get hooked up with Corley and Doane in a sheep-killing deal that wound up in murder?" Sam asked.

Temple didn't answer. He didn't say anything. He didn't move. Sam said: "You're under arrest for the murder of Pete Nickels. Saddle up a horse and come along."

Temple dribbled half a dozen rivets into a box and closed the lid. He tossed the harness to one side as Bud yelled from the corral: "I've got him in my sights, Pa! I can blow him right out of his saddle."

"Put up the rifle," Temple said sternly. "No sense in making a bad situation worse."

Temple strode on past the boy into a corral that held several horses, roped and saddled a mount, and within a matter of minutes rode up beside Sam. He still didn't say anything to Sam. He stared straight ahead, his black mustache bristling, his mouth a tight, bitter line.

"You want to tell me what happened out there at the sheep camp?" Sam asked.

Temple acted as if he hadn't heard. Sam shrugged. He said— "Let's ride."—and started toward town, Temple beside him. The boy stepped out of the corral, just jumpy enough to be dangerous. If the rest of Temple's sons had been home, Sam thought again, it would have been a touchy situation.

"It might make things easier for you if you tell me what happened," Sam said.

Temple still stared straight ahead toward Cañon, his face expressionless. Sam didn't try again. He hoped Faraday would be in his office when he reached the courthouse. If he wasn't, Sam would go to his cabin and wake him. There was a chance that Faraday, with his age and experience, might be able to crack Temple.

They reined up and tied in front of the courthouse. Temple, his head high and back straight, walked ahead of Sam into the sheriff's office. Faraday sat at his desk, looking rested and more like the old Faraday Sam had known all his life. But Sam had no illusions about the sheriff's health. It would take very little to exhaust him again, and once more the thought plagued Sam that Faraday wouldn't be around when this affair came to an end, and Sam knew he needed the older man's advice if nothing else.

"Howdy, Rance," Faraday said, leaning back in his swivel chair.

"Sit down," Sam said, pulling up a chair so Temple would be sitting across the desk from Faraday.

"Will you tell this young idiot of a deputy to let me go?" Temple said between clenched teeth. "I had nothing to do with Pete Nickels' murder if he was murdered."

Sam drew the paper from his pocket that Scotty Doane had signed and, unfolding it, handed it to Faraday who read it, nodded, and slipped it into a desk drawer. He leaned back in his chair again, his hands on the arms of his chair.

"I'm afraid we can't do that," Faraday said. "We have an eyewitness to the boy's murder, so we know that Monk Corley was the one who pulled the trigger. We have reason to think that you and Scotty were persuaded by Monk to go out there to kill sheep, but you had no intention of killing the Nickels boy."

"You seem to know all about it," Temple said.

"We know a good deal," Faraday agreed.

"Well, then," Temple taunted, "if Monk killed the kid, why ain't you got him in the jug?"

"We will," Faraday said. "Right now we're concerned about you, Rance. I hate to see you in this kind of trouble. We've known each other for more years than I like to think about. I know Monk can be purty damn' persuasive when he sets his mind to it, but still I am surprised that he was able to get you into a sheep-killing expedition like he must have done. Scotty Doane, sure. Scotty trails around after Monk like the rest of the ten-cow ranchers, but you don't have to."

"You're real complimentary to a man you're accusing of murder," Temple said bitterly. "Come off it. You don't have an eyewitness. What kind of bull are you giving me?"

"No bull," Faraday said. "Kitty Nickels rode out to the sheep camp to get Pete to come away with her because she was afraid that something would happen to him. We all were, as far as that goes, but we didn't figure it would happen till after Black Mike drove his sheep across the deadline. Now, with the wisdom of hindsight, we know we should have gone out there when Kitty did, or sooner. Anyhow, Kitty was back in the timber and she saw the whole thing."

Temple stared hard at Faraday for several seconds, then he said: "Get me Lee Davis. I've got a right to talk to a lawyer."

"We'll get him," Faraday said. "But it's like Sam told you. If you would give us a written statement telling exactly what happened, it would be better for you all around. You'd be charged with sheep killing, not murder. You know as well as Sam and I do that you ain't going to be found guilty of sheep killing. Chances are the jury would be composed mostly of cattlemen, and there ain't a cowman in the county who ain't sore as hell at Black Mike for raising all this dust in the first place."

"Get me my lawyer," Temple said.

"All right, I said we would." Faraday nodded. "We have Kitty's testimony and we have a statement from Scotty Doane ..."

"That yellow-bellied son-of-a-bitch!" Temple bellowed. "So he made a statement, did he? Monk will kill the bastard."

"I don't think he'll get a chance," Faraday said. "If you will give us a statement, we'll change the charge and Lee Davis will know how to take it from there. It's like I said, Rance. I hate like hell to charge you with murder when it was Monk who ..."

"You've run off at the mouth long enough," Temple said. "Lock me up. Put me in the same cell Scotty's in and you'll really have a murder charge against me."

Faraday shrugged and nodded at Sam. "Put him in the big cell, Sam. Rance, we'll get word to Lee that you want to see him."

Sam took Temple along the corridor to the big cell that was usually used to sober up drunks on Saturday night, but Sam knew what the sheriff was thinking. They could lock Temple and Corley into the same cell, but Doane had to be kept away from them.

When Sam returned to the sheriff's office, Faraday was studying Doane's statement again. He said: "We drew the short one again, Sam. It's like it was with Doc and Augie Pope. Even if we got Augie to talk, it wouldn't count like Doc's testimony would. Right now I ain't sure how far Scotty's statement will take us even if the judge don't throw it out, but Rance's word would go a long ways."

"We're not likely to get anything out of Temple," Sam said.

"That's right," Faraday agreed. "I talked to Scotty just before you got here and he said he'd take the stand and testify, but he may change his mind by the time the trial comes around."

Sam heard horses in the street and moved to the window. Six riders were coming in from the south, Corley and his foreman, Jig Delaney, leading. The other four were MC hands.

"Who is it?" Faraday asked.

"Corley and five of his men," Sam said.

Faraday swore. "That's like Monk. Chances are he hasn't heard that we know anything about it, but he'd show up in town just to let us know we ain't big enough to arrest him if and when we do find out."

Sam didn't say anything for a time. He watched the six men rein up in front of the hotel, dismount, and tie, thinking all the time that he'd never have a better opportunity to take Corley. It would be one way of meeting his challenge, and it would certainly be safer than riding out to the MC. But how could he buck six men? He didn't want to ask Faraday for help, and he wasn't sure how good his help would be anyhow.

Then Sam saw his chance. Delaney and the four cowboys went into the hotel bar and Corley crossed the street to the bank. Sam said—"I'm going after Corley."—and wheeled toward the door.

"No!" Faraday shouted. "Don't get yourself killed, damn it. I can't afford to lose you."

"You're not going to lose me," Sam said. "I'll have him locked up in about five minutes."

He strode out of the courthouse and along the street toward the bank, wondering what his father would do.

XIII

Sam had not been on Main Street any time during the day; he had not talked to any of the townsmen about the murder. He had not even given any thought to how they would react, or even whether they had heard about it. But now as he strode rapidly along the boardwalk, he realized they knew. Knots of men were gathered along the street, some farmers and a few small ranchers and cowboys, but the majority were townsmen—Doc Harvey, Bill Barton who owned the livery stable, druggist Charley Knowles, Abe Kahn who ran the Mercantile, and others including Hoby Stewart who had left the hotel desk to gossip about the murder.

Just before he reached the bank, Sam saw the lawyer, Lee Davis, standing with several ranchers. On impulse Sam stopped and said: "Rance Temple is in jail. He wants to see you."

Apparently none of them had seen Sam bring in Temple and they were surprised, almost as surprised as if he had said Monk Corley was in jail. One of them grabbed Sam's arm, saying: "You're bulling us. You couldn't arrest Rance."

Irritated, Sam jerked loose. "He's in jail and we promised to get word to Lee. It's up to him whether he wants to take the case or not."

"I'll take it," Davis said, and started toward the jail in a long-legged lope as if he were afraid some other lawyer would beat him to Rance Temple.

Sam went on toward the bank, thinking that these men were in a state of shock. Everyone had known that trouble would come out of the cattlemen's deadline and Black Mike Nickels' publicly stated intention of driving his sheep across it. Still, none of them had really been prepared for it when it had come. Or maybe they hadn't been prepared for the way it had come. If it had been an open fight between Black Mike and the cattlemen, and if men had been killed, no one would have been shocked. But it was something else to have it break open before Black Mike had crossed the deadline, and to have Pete Nickels killed the way he was.

At the moment the town's opinion had not crystallized. It would take days, or perhaps only hours. Sam knew very well that he and Ben Faraday might have everyone except Black Mike and the twins against them. Basically Cañon was a cattlemen's town. No one was going to get very excited about Scotty Doane's arrest, but almost everyone would be worked up over Rance Temple and Monk Corley being in jail. Sam had no illusions about the attitude his father would take. The question was how great was Jonas Cassidy's influence. The townsmen might follow him as long as the fight was in the talking stage, but Sam didn't think they would actually try to break Corley and Temple out of jail. If there was that kind of trouble, it would more likely come from the cowboys. In any case, Sam and Faraday would soon know.

He reached the bank and tried the front door. It was locked. He should have known it would be because it was after 4:00 p.m. For a moment he considered pounding on the door, and knew that wasn't the thing to do. His father probably wouldn't open up. Besides, it would attract too much attention. Any unusual commotion might bring the MC men roaring out of the hotel bar and shooting before he could get Corley to the jail. He didn't expect that kind of thing yet, but he couldn't take any chances on provoking it.

The only other alternative was to enter the building through the back door. Usually his father kept it locked, but on a warm afternoon like this, the door would probably be open. He strode around the building, wading through the dog kennel that covered the vacant lot between the bank and the Mercantile. He found that the back door was open as he had expected.

Sam drew his gun and stepped inside. A narrow hall led from the rear of the building to Jonas Cassidy's office. A storeroom was on the left. No one would be in it, and the chances were that no one was in the bank portion of the building except the bookkeeper, Harry Pierce, who was not a man to start anything. Sam moved down the hall, not sure yet what his father would do. He heard Corley say: "It was unfortunate that the Nickels boy was killed. We had no intention of that happening. We thought that if we hit the sheep before they crossed the deadline, we'd nip this thing in the bud and save trouble in the long run."

Corley paused, and then added: "Of course I don't know who it was that did it. We had a meeting at the MC a couple of days ago and agreed on what should be done. I guess some of the boys took it on themselves to actually do it. One of them might have been Scotty Doane. I don't know."

"I think it was nipped in the bud, all right," Jonas said. "Nickels and his boys will get their damned sheep back to where they belong. I don't look for any more trouble now. As for you being involved in that boy's murder, it's simply ridiculous."

Sam wondered how a man as smart as his father was could be so blind. He stepped into the office, his gun lined on Corley. He said: "You're wrong, Dad. The trouble has just started. You're under arrest, Corley, for the murder of Pete Nickels. Unbuckle your gun belt and lay it on the desk, then start down the hall."

Jonas and Corley sat and stared at Sam as if paralyzed. This was sacrilege, something that simply could not be happening. Jonas started to sputter, but Corley interrupted with: "Get this young whelp off my back. I ain't going to his damn' jail."

"You're going, all right," Sam said, "unless you want to get shot right here. If you'd rather try for your gun, go ahead. A dead man will be a lot less trouble to us than a live one."

"I ain't that big a fool," Corley snapped, "with you standing there, holding a gun on me."

"Then do what I tell you," Sam said. "My patience has run short. It got that way when I looked at Pete's body this morning. He was my friend, Corley. I liked him and I can tell you one thing for certain. I'm not going to let his murder go. I wouldn't anyhow, but I've got a personal reason to see that you hang."

"Hang!" Jonas screamed the word. "I don't know why I sent you away to college. They sure didn't teach you anything. Nobody is going to hang Monk Corley. Not after what he's done for this community."

"Come on, Monk," Sam said. "You'll go to jail or I'll shoot you right where you sit."

Corley's dark face had turned as pale as it could under his tan. Probably the thought that he might hang had never occurred to him. He had acted as if he were above the law as long as Sam could remember, and the idea that conditions had changed was enough to shock him into obeying Sam's order. He rose, stripped off his gun belt, laid it on the desk, and turned toward the door. Sam picked up the gun belt and followed Corley out of the office.

"Don't do this, Samuel!" Jonas screamed after them. "You're making the biggest mistake of your life. You'll regret this as long as you ..."

Sam and Corley went on down the hall, Jonas' shrill words becoming just unintelligible sound. They went on through the back door, Sam saying: "Go around the bank to the street and head for the courthouse. When I came by a little while ago, a lot of men were in the street. Don't stop and talk to them or try to start anything if you want to keep living."

"I sure do," Corley said hoarsely, "but, by God, it looks to me like you don't. Before this is over, I'll have Faraday's hide. I'll have yours, too, and I'll nail 'em both up on the front door of the courthouse."

Sam let it go. Corley could make all the threats he wanted to about the future. Sam wanted to lock him up in the jail and that was all he wanted right now. They rounded the corner of the bank and turned along Main Street toward the courthouse. The sight of Sam bringing Corley in at gunpoint caused an involuntary sound to escape from the men along the street. It might have been one of shock, of consternation, or just plain surprise. Sam wasn't sure. He was sure that there wasn't a man on the street who had given him a chance of bringing Monk Corley out of the bank.

"Keep going," Sam said in a low tone. "Don't slow up."

Corley walked with the jerky motion of a toy soldier on a string, but he didn't argue with Sam or try to get anyone to interfere. He held his head high, his arms swinging at his sides, his boot heels clicking on the boards of the walk. They moved past Doc Harvey and Abe Kahn and Bill Barton and others. No one said a word. Corley looked straight ahead. The men on the street stared at him, and then as Corley reached them, they looked away as if they were suddenly uneasy at being caught staring curiously at a man whose word had been law as long as most of them could remember.

Sam and Corley reached the end of the block and crossed the street, then followed the path that angled through the weeds to the front door of the courthouse. They climbed the spur-scarred steps and went through the door and into the narrow hall, then turned left into the sheriff's office.

Ben Faraday sat at his desk. He rose when he saw Corley come in. He said: "Sam told me he'd fetch you in five minutes. I think he took a little longer."

"Sorry to make you wait so long," Sam said. "What was it, six minutes?"

"Just about." Faraday winked at Sam, his face masked against the humor that sparkled in his eyes. "Go on in, Monk. Lee Davis and Rance Temple are having a talk. It will interest you, too, I think."

"Rance?" The name was jolted out of Corley. "I don't believe he's in jail."

"Show him." Faraday tossed a ring of keys to Sam. "I don't have to lie to you about anything, Monk. I never did. I thought you knew that."

Corley was visibly shaken. He swallowed, and managed to say: "That's right, Ben. You never did, but there is something you'd better know. I've never been in jail in my life. If you lock me up in that stinking hole now, I'll get you. I don't know how, but I will. Both you and this smart-aleck bastard you've got doing your dirty work for you."

"There's been times when you've scared me," Faraday said, "but not any more. You put the rope on your own neck when you pulled the trigger on the Nickels boy. Lock him up, Sam."

Opening the door of the corridor, Sam went back into the jail and unlocked the door of the big cell. Temple and Davis were inside. When they saw Corley come slowly into the corridor, then move even more slowly along it until he reached the cell, they looked as shocked as the men on the street had a few minutes before.

Corley stepped inside, saying: "I guess you can get us out of here in a hurry, Lee."

"No," Davis said uneasily. "I can't. Not on a murder charge."

Sam locked the door behind Corley. He didn't glance at Scotty Doane who was alone in a small cell across the corridor. He didn't want to see him. The little man would be scared, so scared that he would probably promise not to testify on the stand and to renounce the statement he had made.

Returning to the sheriff's office, Sam said: "The mighty have fallen. No one really believes it yet, not even after seeing me take him along the street."

"They will," Faraday said. "It just takes a little time." He shook his head, smiling. "You're a cool one, boy. I thought you were committing suicide when you went after Monk."

"It might come to that yet," Sam said.

"We've got him and we'll keep him," Faraday said, "but we'll have to watch out for Jig Delaney and his MC boys. Maybe they won't try anything today, but they'll be along."

Sam had moved to the window to look into the street. He said softly: "It's today, Ben. They're headed here."

XIV

For a few seconds Ben Faraday sat frozen, then he asked: "How many?"

"Five."

"This is it," Faraday said. "I was hoping they'd give us a little time. I figured we might get help from somewhere."

He rose and crossed to the gun rack. Taking down a .30-30, he checked to see that it was loaded, and handed it to Sam. "Better drop a box of shells into your pocket. I don't think we'll need them, but if things begin to pop, you won't have time to come into the office to get them. You'll find a full box in the top drawer of the desk."

Sam wheeled to the desk, opened the drawer, and, picking up the box of shells, slipped it into his pocket. Faraday took a double-barrel shotgun from the rack, broke it, and saw it was loaded, then quickly came to the desk and, taking a handful of shotgun shells from the drawer, dropped them into his pocket.

"Come on," he said. "The trick is to keep 'em outside. You never like to shoot a man in a situation like this, but it's better to shoot them than let them shoot us. Don't forget they are breaking the law. Or aim to, and will if we let 'em."

Sam followed him out of the office and through the hall to the front door, thinking that Faraday was like an old war horse. He was sick and near death, but he forgot all that when a situation like this faced them. Sam had never admired Ben Faraday as much as he did at this moment, standing beside him with Jig Delaney and the four MC riders not more than fifty feet away.

"That's close enough, Jig," Faraday said, pointing the shotgun at him. "The shells in this gun are loaded with buckshot. At this distance they'll put a hole in you I can stick my arm through and I'll have a shell left over for any of the others who think they can get a gun out of leather fast enough to cut me down before I pull the trigger a second time."

The MC men stopped as Sam's rifle, held at his hip, centered on Slim Goble, the cowhand who stood on the left of the semicircle the five men had formed in front of the courthouse steps. Aside from Jig Delaney who had ramrodded the MC for ten years or more, Goble was the only one of the five Sam knew, a chunky man in his late twenties. He had been raised in the county and had started riding for Corley before Sam had gone to college. He had a reputation as being a tough hand. The other three were drifters, probably hired in the spring.

For all Sam knew, these three might be as tough as Goble, but if Sam and Faraday took Goble and Delaney out of the fight, the other three wouldn't push it. At least that was Sam's guess, so he kept his eyes on Goble, the rifle barrel pointing squarely at his chest.

Jig Delaney spat contemptuously in Faraday's direction. He said: "For an old man, Ben, you sure are taking long steps."

"I always have, Jig," Faraday said. "Any reason I should stop now?"

"Sure is," Delaney said. "When one of your long steps winds up on Monk Corley's toe, its just too damned long."

"It's Monk's own fault if he got his toe stepped on," Faraday said. "He can't expect to murder a boy and have me look the other way."

"He didn't murder no boy," Delaney said sharply. "Him and me and Rance Temple was playing poker last night at the MC. That's all the alibi he oughta need."

Faraday grinned. "Yep. It's all he oughta need, Jig, but you know and I know it ain't enough."

"Why ain't it?"

"Because he wasn't playing poker with you and Rance last night."

"You making out I'm a liar?" Delaney demanded angrily.

"That's exactly what I'm doing," Faraday said. "You'd lie any day in the year for Monk Corley."

Sam shot the foreman a glance and quickly brought his gaze back to Goble. Delaney was a string bean of a man with a lean, weathered face that looked nearly as hard as one of the tall rocks that marked the edge of the bench where it broke off into the desert east of town. Delaney didn't have to prove he was a good man with his fists or his gun. He had proved it a long time ago in roundup camps, in saloons, and on the streets of Cañon. Sam didn't think he'd stand still for Faraday calling him a liar, but to his surprise, Delaney's thin-lipped mouth curled up into a grin.

"Well now, maybe I would, Ben," he said, "but that ain't what we came for. We're here to see Monk. I figger you're going to hold him for a while and I'd like to know what he wants done."

"All right, shuck your gun belts," Faraday said. "I'll let you go in one at a time to see him. You can start, Jig."

"Oh, we ain't giving up our guns," Delaney said. "You don't really expect us to, do you?"

"No, I don't," Faraday said, "but then I don't expect you to see Monk. I guess I look kind of stupid, but I ain't *that* stupid. You're a good cowman, Jig. You've done more to make the MC what it is than Monk has, and you'll do real good without asking Monk anything."

Again Sam shot a glance at Delaney. This time the man's thin face held no trace of a grin. It was all he could do to keep from pulling his gun, but he didn't lose his head completely because he knew Ben Faraday would do exactly what he said.

"All right, we won't see Monk today," Delaney ground out, "but we'll be back and next time we'll have an army. We'll take your goddamned courthouse apart, and we'll fill you and your college boy full of holes and take Monk out of there."

"Any time you want to try it, Jig," Faraday said. "Any time."

"Come on," Delaney said. "Let's get out of here."

He turned on his heel. Sam looked at him, not expecting this, and in that moment came close to getting killed. When he brought his gaze back to Goble, the man was sweeping his gun out of leather. Sam fired, the slug catching Goble in his right arm and slamming him around, his gun dropping into the weeds. He let out a squall of pain, and yelled: "He shot me. Damn him, he shot me. Go get Doc!"

"That's right," Sam said. "Take him to the doc, Jig. Leave his gun where it is. He can get it later."

Delaney whirled back to face Sam. He started to curse him, and stopped only when Faraday said: "That's all, Jig. Shut up or I'll shut you up. Slim should have got it in the brisket. That's what he'd have given Sam."

"Come on, come on," Delaney said. "We'll find Doc."

They strode away, Goble lurching and almost falling before Delaney took his arm and steadied him. A moment later they disappeared along Main Street.

Faraday sighed. "It's over for this time, but I figure they'll be back just like he said, and with an army."

Sam stepped to the ground and picked up the .45 Goble had dropped. When he was back beside Faraday again, he asked: "Where do we get that help you were looking for?"

"I wish I knew," the sheriff said wearily. "I'm going to sit down."

He went into his office, placed the shotgun in the gun rack, and dropped into his chair at his desk. Sam put the Winchester back, then said: "Why don't you lie down a while? I don't look for any more trouble tonight."

"No, I don't, either," Faraday said, "but I think I'll sit here a while before I go."

He was all in, Sam saw, and told himself that Faraday would rise to the occasion and then have to pay for it later. For a moment Sam was afraid, more afraid than he had even been before in his life. He wasn't afraid to face and fight a man like Jig Delaney, but he was afraid that he lacked the experience it took to handle a situation such as the one Faraday had just handled.

Faraday wiped the sweat off his face and said glumly: "I dunno, Sam. I used to figger I was a purty good man, but I just don't have the skookum any more."

Sam couldn't tell him he was afraid he wouldn't live long enough to see this through to the end, so he said: "You're still a good man in my book, Ben. I was just thinking I wished I was half as good."

"Well, now," Faraday said, a trace of a smile coming to the corners of his mouth, "I thought you were."

XV

Faraday went to his cabin to rest and did not return to his office until dusk. He said: "Go get your supper, Sam. I'll be all right for a while, but maybe you ought to sleep here. There's a cot in that storeroom yonder and plenty of blankets. I've done that many times when I didn't have a deputy."

"All right," Sam said. "Somebody's got to be here. I don't think I'll be sleeping at home from now on."

As he left the courthouse, he glanced along Main Street and saw that it was deserted. Probably there would be no trouble tonight. Maybe it wouldn't come at night at all. This, of course, was part of the problem. Neither he nor Faraday could even guess when it would come. All they could be certain of was that it would come.

When he reached his home, he saw that the kitchen was empty, but he heard someone upstairs. He called: "Ma?"

"Up here, Samuel," she answered. "In the bedroom."

He took the stairs two at a time and stopped in the doorway of his parents' bedroom. His mother had two suitcases open on the bed, both of them packed and ready to close. When she saw Sam in the doorway, she sat down in her rocking chair and blew her nose. She had been crying. He just stood there and looked at her, thinking that this was the first time he had ever seen her cry.

She wiped her eyes, and said: "This is a sorry occasion, Samuel. There's been many a time when I have thought of leaving your father, but it never quite came to that. I guess in some ways I've had a good life. At least I've had a roof over my head and I've had enough to eat."

She stopped and looked down at her folded hands that were on her lap. "But I've never been myself. I guess every idea I've had came from your father. Now I'm going to move into the hotel and look for work. I don't know what I'll do if I can't find something because I don't have any money. Your father, you know, never let me have any."

"What caused this?" Sam asked. "I mean, what was the last straw?"

"He came home from the bank this afternoon in a terrible temper," she said. "He called you names and said that after all he'd done for you, you wouldn't obey him. He was mad mostly because you had arrested Monk Corley." She rose and closed the suitcases. "Kitty was still here. He said she couldn't stay. He was going to the hotel for his supper and he didn't want her in the house when he got back. I told him I was going, too, and he said that was fine."

"Where's Kitty now?"

"In the hotel. We cooked supper before she left so we wouldn't have to eat there. All she has is the money you gave her."

"Don't worry," he said. "I'll borrow some money from Ben. I'll rent a house as soon as I can. You'll be all right."

"Of course," she said, looking around the room as if she would never see it again. "The Lord will provide."

Sam picked up the suitcases. They left the room and went down the stairs. She stopped in the living room and again looked around. Then, tight-lipped, she walked out of the house. Sam stayed with her until she registered and Hoby Stewart, bursting to tell this new happening to someone, gave her a key, and Sam carried her suitcases upstairs. He shook his head as he glanced around the room. It was a poor place to call home, he thought, and this was what both Kitty and his mother would have to do for a while.

"You try to sleep," he said. "I'll see you tomorrow."

"Of course, Samuel," she said. "Thank you."

He went downstairs to the dining room. As he ate supper, he thought about his father. He had never considered Jonas Cassidy much of a man, but now he realized how small and petty he really was, yet this was not the way people in the community pictured him. He was not surprised when his father came into the dining room just as he was finishing his pie. Jonas walked to his table and sat down across from him, his face dark, almost purple. Sam thought he had the appearance of a man who was about to have a stroke. He had seen his father look like this before when he was very angry, but this was the worst.

"I've been looking for you," Jonas said. "I went to the jail and Faraday told me you might be here." He was a man who always tried to hide his emotion, if he had any. Sometimes Sam thought anger was the only emotion he was capable of feeling. Now he spoke in the clipped way he had when he was grappling with something he couldn't quite handle.

He cleared his throat. "I think I had better make my position clear to you at the outset. I realize you are a grown man. Still, I had expected you to consider my wishes in regard to the work you chose. You did not. I still expected you to conduct yourself in a manner that befitted my son. You chose not to do that when you arrested Monk Corley. For you to even consider suspecting Monk of the murder of the Nickels boy is ... is beyond my understanding."

During his growing up years, Sam had never been sure how sincere his father was in what he believed and said, but now, aware of the tension that gripped Jonas, of the sense of outrage over Corley's arrest, Sam decided this time he was honest in what he was saying. Maybe it was because he had to believe in Corley's innocence. Otherwise, nothing was left for him to believe in.

"I'm sure this is not new to you," Jonas went on, "but what I am going to say now is new. If you change your mind, perhaps I will change mine. I'm having a new will drawn up which leaves one silver dollar to you. No more. And if you go on this way, I venture to say that Judge Murray will not have room in his office for you."

Sam leaned back in his chair. He wanted to laugh, to stand up and let out a great bellow of relief. For the first time in his life he was a free man. In these few minutes his father had set him free from the natural debt a son owes his father.

But he did not laugh or shout in relief. He merely said: "All right, Dad, if that's the way you want it."

"That's the way I want it unless you change your mind and persuade Faraday to release Monk," his father said.

"No, I couldn't do that."

"Very well," Jonas said. "One more thing. I will see to it that Ben Faraday is never elected sheriff in this county again."

That was an idle threat, Sam thought, in view of Faraday's health, but apparently his father had not heard about that. Sam said: "There is one thing, Dad. As a banker, you would want a good man in the sheriff's office, it seems to me. Once the fabric of law and order is torn ..."

Jonas rose. "College talk," he said savagely. "Law and order depends upon decent men not being arrested because of the whim of an inexperienced deputy or a sick old man."

He walked out of the dining room. He had learned during his years as a banker that the power to give money and take away money was a tool he could use to get his way. Now he was disappointed that his formula had not worked with his son.

When Sam returned to the sheriff's office, he said: "Ben, my father has just disinherited me, unless I can persuade you to release Corley."

Faraday's eyes searched Sam's face for a moment, then he said: "I'm sorry I got you into this. I didn't ..."

"Don't be sorry," Sam said. "It's the way I want it. Now Dad won't bother to give me orders. He also said he would see to it that you will not run for sheriff next time."

"I'm afraid the good Lord is going to beat him to that one," Faraday said. "Well, I'm going home. Lock the courthouse door after me. That way nobody will get in without you knowing it. I don't expect you to stay awake all night."

"I'm not going to stay awake," Sam said. "I didn't have much sleep last night."

Still, he found sleep evasive. He would fall asleep and wake up and hear the courthouse creak and groan under the impact of the night wind, and then he would drop off only to wake again. When it was daylight, he got up and dressed, feeling as if he had not slept at all.

XVI

Sam unlocked the front door of the courthouse and stood in front of the building, enjoying the early morning sunshine. For the moment the day was quiet and peaceful. It would be warm again, but now it was pleasantly cool. He could not see a cloud anywhere except along the crest of the Bearpaws. He wondered if Black Mike would have the funeral today. Probably he would, as warm as the last two days had been.

He was still standing there when Tommy Riggs, who worked for the hotel, arrived with breakfast for the prisoners. Sam helped the boy with the trays, finding Rance Temple sullenly silent and Monk Corley running off at the mouth with threats and curses.

"You ready to make a statement, Rance?" Sam asked.

Temple didn't even look up from his place but kept on eating.

Sam asked: "How about you, Monk? It'll be easier on everybody if you do."

"Easier for you and Faraday to hang me if I say what you want me to say," Corley snapped, then he laughed. "Sure, I'll make a statement. I was home all that night. I went to bed early. Bring me some paper and I'll write it out and sign it."

"We don't want a statement unless it's the truth," Sam said. "I understood you were playing poker with Rance and Jig Delaney."

That threw Corley off stride for a moment, then he recovered and said quickly: "That's right, ain't it, Rance?"

Temple, his mouth full, mumbled something about it being right. Sam said: "Your story doesn't hang together. You just said you went to bed early."

"It hangs together, all right." Corley laughed again. "We quit early. Then I went to bed."

Sam turned away, thinking he had not expected anything out of either of them. Corley called after him: "You'll never keep me in this stinking hole. Jig will have me out of here before dark." He laughed, a taunting, contemptuous sound. "Or do you figure you can hold me?"

Sam kept on walking and didn't answer. There was no use to tell him Jig had tried and failed. Corley would say Jig would try again, and Sam didn't doubt that he would.

Scotty Doane whispered: "Cassidy."

He had his face pressed against the door of his cell, his hands clutching the bars on both sides of his face. When Sam turned to him, he said in a low tone: "They're gonna kill me. I knew they would. Monk, he says that Jig and a lot of others are gonna break him out and they'll kill me while they're doing it. You've got to get me out of here."

Sam hesitated, knowing this could happen, and he saw no point in lying to Doane by saying it wouldn't. Instead, he said: "You're safer in jail than out, Scotty."

"No I ain't," Doane said. "I'd be hard to find if I was out. In here it'd be like shooting fish in a barrel."

Sam shook his head. "I'll talk to Ben, but I don't see how we can let you out. Let them talk. I think you'll be safe in here. Jig tried to get in here yesterday just after we locked Corley up, but he didn't make it. All I can tell you is that they'll have to kill me before they can get at you."

"That ain't no comfort," Doane said. "Not a damned bit."

Sam went on into the office, closing the corridor door. Tommy Riggs was waiting for him. "You don't have to wait," Sam said. "There's last night's supper dishes. Take them, and when you come at noon, you can take the breakfast dishes."

"I waited to talk to you," the boy said. "There's something you ought to know." He glanced at the corridor door and lowered his voice. "A couple of hardcases came in last night. They had dinner in the dining room, and then went into the bar. I overheard 'em. I guess they wanted to be overheard the way they was talking. Maybe they wanted you to know. Anyhow, they said they was gonna kill you today."

"You know their names?"

"They was strangers, but like I said, they're hardcases. It don't take nobody smart to see that. They just kind of buffaloed everybody like they thought they was it. One of 'em is a big man. Big as Black Mike Nickels. Or Mister Corley. The other one is kind of little. The small one called the big one Smoky."

Sam knew, then. They were the men who had stopped the stage on the pass and tried to keep him from coming to Cañon. He said: "Thanks, Tommy. I'll watch out for them."

"When I had a chance to sneak back of the desk, I looked at the register," Tommy said. "Hoby won't let me do that. Says it ain't none of my business who's registered and who ain't. Anyhow, they signed their names Smoky Rash and Trigger Moore and said Cheyenne was their home. That's all I know about 'em, Mister Cassidy."

"Thanks, Tommy," Sam said again.

The boy gathered up the previous night's dinner dishes and left. Sam was still sitting at the desk when Ben Faraday came in. Looking at him, Sam thought the sheriff seemed a little more frail than he had the day before.

"I hate to bother you," Sam said, "but I need some money. Ma and Kitty both have left home and neither one of 'em's got a nickel. I gave Kitty all I had. If you could loan me ..."

"Sure I can," Faraday said. "They say you can't take it with you to where I'm going." He drew a handful of coins from his pocket. "I've only got $20 and a little silver here, but I'll get some out of the bank if you need it."

"Twenty dollars is enough for now," Sam said. "Dad would be sore if he knew you were taking it out of the bank to give to us."

Faraday laughed. "What he don't know ain't gonna hurt him. Go get your breakfast."

When he was in the hall, Sam checked his gun. He had no way of knowing when the two men would jump him, or where. Tommy was right in saying they were hardcases, but whether they were fast with their guns was another matter. Men who were really fast did not have to make any claims about how fast they were, and picking names like Smoky and Trigger made Sam think they were like a great many so-called badmen, more bluff than anything else, building up a fake reputation and then living by it. He hadn't mentioned them to Faraday, but he would when he came back. The sheriff might know how good they were.

He did not find either Kitty or his mother in the dining room, and after he'd finished breakfast, he asked Hoby Stewart if they were in their rooms. Stewart shook his head and looked wise and said: "They left about half an hour ago. Didn't even get their breakfast."

Sam found this hard to believe. He asked: "Where did they go?"

Stewart didn't look as wise then. He said: "They didn't say."

Sam thought about this as he walked back to the courthouse. He was sure they would not have returned to the Cassidy house. Jonas might change his mind in time when he got tired of hotel food and keeping house. He had never been a man who could look after himself, but it would take a few days to convince him that his comfort was more important than his principles. It was possible, of course, that they had found work, but it seemed unlikely that it would happen in this short time. When he went into the sheriff's office, he found Black Mike Nickels standing in front of Faraday's desk. He turned when he heard Sam's footsteps and nodded and said: "'Morning, Sam."

Sam nodded back. "Howdy, Mike," he said, and waited.

The sheepman's presence needed an explanation. After the way he had talked the morning he had seen Pete's body, Sam had never expected to see him here. Too, he had been as cocky and domineering in his way as Monk Corley had in his, but now he looked neither cocky nor domineering. He stared at the floor as if he were a thoroughly beaten man, red-faced and embarrassed as he twisted his hat in his hands.

"The funeral's this afternoon at two," he said. "I hope you can come. Faraday says he'll stay here while you're gone."

"I'll be there," Sam said.

"Good." Nickels glanced up and swallowed and looked at the floor again. "I've changed my mind about almost everything since I found out about Pete. The twins are with what's left of the sheep. We lost about five hundred head. I didn't really figure you fellows would arrest the three bastards that done the killing, but I looked there just now, and, by God, all three of 'em are in jail."

"We've done all we can," Sam said. "Whether a jury in this county will convict any of them is another question."

"Like you say, you done all you could," Black Mike said. "I came to tell you that I ain't getting between you and Kitty no more. If you kids want to get married today, it's fine with me."

This was the last thing Sam expected to hear. He had thought his own father would give way before Black Mike would, but Jonas had not had a son murdered. Perhaps that and his sense of guilt about it were what had humbled Black Mike Nickels.

"I'm glad to hear that," Sam said. "We'll wait a few days, of course."

"Kitty and your ma are in my house," Black Mike went on. "I got Kitty out of bed early to tell her and she wanted your ma to come, too, which was all right with me since she left your pa. I told her to stay as long as she wanted."

This, then, was the answer to where his mother and Kitty had gone. It was as unexpected as Black Mike's blessing on their marriage. "Thanks," Sam said. "I've been worried about where Ma would stay. The hotel isn't much good after a day or two."

"I'm glad to have her," Nickels said. "Oh, there was one more thing. Them toughs that Corley had stationed up there on the pass are in town and talking about gunning you down. If you need any help, just holler."

"I'll keep my eyes open," Sam said. "I believe in a man stomping his own snakes."

"So do I," Black Mike said, "but two snakes are too much for a man to handle at one time,"

He walked out of the office, bent-shouldered, his gaze on the floor. He might in the future be as bull-headed and domineering as he had in the past, but for the moment at least he was in the valley of the shadow and Sam had a feeling he would never be the same again.

"You don't seem to be much surprised about having these men on your tail," Faraday said.

"I already knew about them," Sam said. "Are they as tough as Corley thinks?"

"You never know for sure about men like that until they stand up to you," Faraday said, "but from what I hear, Trigger Moore is. Rash ain't. He's a big stupid bully who does what Moore says. Now let's get one thing straight. If you need any help, I'm the man to give it."

"I'll remember," Sam said.

He didn't argue with Faraday, but what Sam had said to Black Mike still held. A man had to stomp his own snakes.

XVII

Sam was in the sheriff's office when Tommy Riggs arrived with the prisoners' noon meals. Faraday asked: "What room did Hoby Stewart give them two toughs?"

The boy looked surprised, then he answered: "Room Twenty. Why?"

Faraday scowled thoughtfully, then he said: "I ain't been upstairs in the hotel for a long time. Where is Room Twenty?"

"One of the corner rooms in the front."

Faraday nodded as if that was exactly what he expected. "Did they ask for that room? Or one in that position?"

Tommy frowned and scratched his head and finally nodded. "Yeah, I guess they did. I didn't pay it no heed 'cause most folks like the rooms that are in front 'cause there's more to see. They like the corner ones in the summer 'cause they're cooler with a wind blowing through the room when they open both windows."

"They probably paid Hoby a little extra, maybe," Faraday suggested.

"I wasn't aiming to say that," Tommy muttered uneasily, glancing away. "Hoby can sure be mean when he sets his mind to it, so I don't tattle on him, but he holds them two front corner rooms back and pretends they're full unless he gets paid another dollar. I didn't see them two hardcases pay him his dollar, but chances are they did or he'd have said they was taken."

Faraday nodded as if that was what he had thought all the time. He said: "Sam, go get your dinner and then go to the funeral. I'll be all right till you come back."

"What's all the questions for, Ben?" Sam asked.

"Oh, I was just curious about where them two sidewinders had holed up," Faraday said casually, too casually, Sam thought. "When you get done eating dinner, I want you to go on to Room Twenty. If them two plug-uglies are there, tell 'em to get out of town by six this evening, that it's an order from the sheriff's office. But don't start a fight with them."

"I don't see the sense in stirring up a hornet's nest," Sam said. "Maybe they won't bother me if I don't bother them."

Faraday shook his head. "You don't know men of that caliber. They always figure to stack the deck so the good hands fall to them. This way we get the jump on 'em and it'll worry 'em. Now do what I tell you."

As Sam ate his dinner, he noted that neither Rash nor Moore was in the dining room. When he finished, he went upstairs, found Room Twenty, and knocked. The small man, Trigger Moore, opened the door. Startled, he stepped back and started to reach for his gun, then froze, his right hand splayed over the butt of his .45.

"Hold it," Sam said quickly. "I'm not here to start a fight, so don't pull your iron. I came to tell you to be out of town by six this evening. That's an order from the sheriff's office."

The big man, Smoky Rash, was on his feet across the room. Moore glanced at him, and then back at Sam. Now for the first time Sam understood Faraday's tactics. He couldn't tell whether the two men were scared, but it was plain they were surprised and a little upset at least.

"We ain't broke no laws," Moore said. "This is a pretty high-handed order, seems to me."

"I guess it is," Sam said, "but the sheriff's got plenty of reason, so do what you're told and there won't be any trouble."

Both men laughed, a little uneasily, Sam thought, then Moore said: "I don't think we're gonna obey any tin-star sheriff's order and you can tell him that. You handled us pretty good up on the pass, bucko, but you'll never do it again."

"We'll see," Sam said. "You've been warned. That's all I was told to do."

Smoky Rash crossed the room to stand beside Moore. "Listen, you young squirt. There never was a day when the likes of you could order men like us around. At six o'clock I'm going to be down there on Main Street, looking for you. If you don't have a yellow streak a foot wide down your back, you'll be there, too."

"I'll be there," Sam said, and, turning on his heel, strode down the hall.

As he walked toward the church, he thought about this. If Trigger Moore was the faster man with a gun, why was Rash meeting him in the street? It should have been Moore. They had some kind of a trick up their sleeve, but Sam couldn't guess what it was. Maybe Moore was figuring to cut him down from an alley or from the window of his hotel room, but such a scheme was so obvious it seemed stupid and he discarded it immediately.

When he reached the church and saw the rigs tied in front on both sides of the hearse, he told himself there were more people here than he had expected. Black Mike Nickels had few friends in the county, but Pete had gone to high school in Cañon and he and Kitty did have friends. Besides, the manner of his death had created a great deal of sympathy.

For a moment Sam stood in the church doorway and thought there wasn't a vacant seat in the room, then he saw Black Mike and Kitty were sitting in the front row. He walked down the aisle, hoping they could squeeze over enough to give him room to sit beside Kitty. When he reached the end of their pew, he saw that his mother was sitting on the other side of Black Mike.

When Kitty looked up and saw who it was, she tried to smile, but her face was frozen in sorrow. She scooted over against her father who, in turn, moved against Mrs. Cassidy, and enough space opened up on the end of the seat for Sam to sit down. The instant he dropped down beside her, Kitty reached for his hand and held it through the service. The room was very quiet, with no sound except that of people's breathing and the buzzing of a fly against one of the windows. The casket in the front of the room had several bouquets of purple flags and French pinks, and one of wildflowers that Kitty had probably gathered that morning.

Sam remembered Kitty used to go with Pete every spring to pick wildflowers because they both loved them. It had always seemed to Sam to be a feminine trait in Pete, but now it didn't strike him that way. Rather, it seemed to him that it was an indication of the boy's natural gentleness, his love of beauty, and was what had set him apart from Black Mike and the twins.

At exactly 2:00 p.m. the preacher, Ross Fleming, rose and moved to the pulpit. He was a tall, thin man who usually thundered at his congregation with accusations of sin and the promise of a punishment in a fiery hell, but today his voice was low and choked with emotion. Pete had been a regular church-goer, and Sam was certain that Fleming had been genuinely fond of the boy.

The preacher read a short sketch of Pete's life, the usual scripture about many mansions, and then prayed. After he finished, he sat down and the ladies' quartet that sang at the morning church service stood beside the casket and sang two hymns. The preacher rose and moved back to the pulpit again, and Sam was surprised that there was no mention of hell in his sermon. Several times he stopped and wiped his eyes and blew his nose, then went on. Fleming talked about Jesus going and preparing a place for people like Pete Nickels who had been cut down in the budding of manhood, a boy of great promise. Then for the first time he thundered at his audience, demanding why such a crime had been committed? He answered his own question; he said it was greed and selfishness and the struggle for power. It was a crime, he shouted, for which there was no excuse in the eyes of God or man.

The preacher sat down and wiped his face, the corners of his mouth quivering. After a minute or so of absolute silence, Charley Knowles, the druggist who also doubled as undertaker, rose and lifted the lid of the casket. The audience filed past to have one last look at Pete Nickels, and finally no one was left except Knowles, the boys who had been Pete's friends and were serving as pallbearers, and Sam and the three who sat in the pew with him.

Sam rose and, still holding Kitty's hand, walked to the casket and looked down at Pete. Charley Knowles had worked hard, but he failed to make this body resemble the Pete Nickels Sam had known. Suddenly he was filled with so much hatred for Monk Corley that he turned away, his heart pounding, his body tense. More than anything else he wanted to go back to the jail and kill Corley.

He rode to the graveyard with Kitty, his mother, and Black Mike in the hack that Black Mike had rented from the livery stable. They stood beside the grave under the hot sun for a short service, and Sam found the lump in his throat so big that it was impossible to swallow. Tears rolled down Black Mike's cheeks, something Sam had seen only once before when Black Mike saw Pete's body. Mrs. Cassidy cried silently, but Kitty did not, and Sam, glancing at her, thought she was cried out. He wished he had been able to spend more time with her these last hours, to give her what comfort he could.

When the graveside service was over, he led Kitty away before the first clod struck the casket. They rode back to the Nickels house in silence, then Black Mike said hoarsely: "I'll take the rig to the stable, then I'm going to ride out to the sheep camp to see how the boys are getting along. You send for me if you need me, Sam."

"I will," Sam said as he stepped down and gave Kitty a hand, and then helped his mother down.

He walked beside Kitty and his mother to the front door. Mrs. Cassidy said: "I'll be here for a few days, Samuel. I don't know how long."

"I'm glad you got a place to stay," he said.

She went inside. Sam looked down at Kitty and said: "I wish I could be with you, but I can't for a while. I don't know what's going to happen."

"I know, I know," she whispered, and then she cried out—"Sam, Sam!"—and buried her face against the front of his shirt.

He held her for a time, then she drew back and said she was all right, he could go now. He kissed her and, turning, walked rapidly back to the courthouse. The sheriff's office was empty. Faraday had gone home to rest, he supposed.

He opened the corridor door and said in a voice that did not sound like his: "Corley, I've just come from Pete's funeral. If there ever was a fiery hell waiting for a man, by God, it's sure waiting for you."

He slammed the heavy door shut, trembling, knowing he could not stay there overnight or he would kill the man. He sat down at the desk to wait for 6:00 p.m.

XVIII

Faraday had not returned to the sheriff's office by 5:56. Sam could not wait any longer. He checked his gun carefully, not wanting to leave the office unguarded, but knowing there was nothing else he could do. He eased the revolver back into the holster, the thought occurring to him that this might be a scheme to break Corley and Rance Temple out of jail while no one was here, but he dismissed the notion immediately. Nobody, and that certainly included Moore and Rash, would know that the office was empty.

As he stepped into the hall, he glanced toward the door, hoping he would see Faraday come in. Then, reaching the doorway, he looked again for Faraday, but the sheriff was not in sight. As he strode toward Main Street, the possibility that Ben Faraday had died alone in his cabin plagued Sam. He could not rid himself of this nagging fear. Faraday's failure to appear on time was not like him.

Then Sam reached Main Street, the sun behind him, his long shadow stretching ahead of him. Smoky Rash waited at the other end of the block, a formidable man who had every intention of killing him. He had no time now to think of Ben Faraday. Only Smoky Rash was important. He could not even think of Trigger Moore. Sam's life depended on drawing faster and shooting straighter than Rash. By some miracle the street was deserted except for the two of them, one Dominick rooster that was scratching in the horse manure in front of the livery stable, and a mangy pup sleeping in the warm, evening sunshine. So the word had got around, probably by virtue of Hoby Stewart's wagging tongue.

Sam had been afraid as he'd sat waiting in the sheriff's office. When he had been a small boy, he had seen a fight here on Cañon's main street. He was supposed to be home, but he had sneaked out and crawled along the narrow space between the Mercantile and the bank. From that vantage point he had seen two cowboys shoot it out, one of them going down with a bullet hole in his thigh. He remembered seeing the blood pump out of the wound and make a dark pool in the gray dust of the street; he remembered seeing men carry the cowboy to Doc Harvey's office and later hearing that the man had died.

That had happened a long time ago, and as far as he knew there had not been a street fight in Cañon since. Now he sensed that people were watching from every window and doorway that faced Main Street just as people had once watched fights to the death between gladiators in ancient Rome or between knights in the Middle Ages. It did not occur to these people, he thought bitterly, that he was the only man who was willing and capable of maintaining law and order in the county.

Rash was moving toward him, little puffs of dust rising from the street each time he took a step. Sam began to pace toward Rash, watching the man for the first hint that he was starting his draw. The fear that had been in Sam a few minutes before was gone. Rash wasn't worried about facing the sun; he wasn't worried about how fast this young deputy was. At least that was the way Sam judged him, for his expression was one of complete, even arrogant, confidence.

Sam remembered what Moore had said in the hotel room: *You handled us pretty good up on the pass, bucko, but you'll never do it again.* From Rash's expression, Sam guessed that was exactly the way he felt.

One moment there was this strained, tense silence that lay upon Main Street, the lengthening shadows reaching across the dust strip, the two men warily approaching each other, then the crack of a rifle broke the silence. Sam had expected Trigger Moore to show up somewhere, but Moore had not fired that shot. Sam was still on his feet and he wouldn't have been if Moore had fired at him. Too, he saw Rash stop abruptly, his expression of smug confidence giving way to one of consternation and fear. Then Rash yanked his gun from leather and started toward Sam in a wild, headlong run, firing as he came.

The first shot was wild, going over Sam's head by a good three feet. The second kicked up a geyser of dust in front of him. Now Rash, realizing how stupid he had been, stopped and leveled his gun, this time taking aim. Rash never got the shot off. Sam, too, had stopped and made his draw. He fired just before Rash squeezed off his third shot. The big man went down, his hat falling off his head, the dust making a white fog around him.

Sam moved slowly toward Rash, his gun cocked. He watched the man pull himself to his knees, saw him lift his gun again. Blood dribbled down his chin from the corners of his mouth; his gun wobbled for a moment, then steadied. Sam didn't wait. He fired a second time, and then a third. Rash fell forward, his face in the dust, and died as the sound of a gunshot rolled along the street.

From somewhere behind Sam, Ben Faraday called: "Upstairs! In the hotel. I think I got Moore, but you'd better look."

Sam whirled. Ben Faraday leaned against the front of the drugstore, his Winchester propped against the wall beside him. He must have been hiding somewhere along the side of the drugstore, far enough back from the street so that neither Sam nor Trigger Moore had seen him. Sam understood it now, understood it as plainly as if someone had drawn a diagram of the plan.

He ran toward the hotel door, knowing that Moore had intended to fire just as Rash pulled the trigger or a second before.

The people behind the windows and in the doorways were watching Sam and Rash in the street. The odds were that no one would have seen Moore fire, or even figure out what had happened until the two killers were miles out of town. Sam plunged into the lobby, spinning an astonished Hoby Stewart out of his path, and went up the stairs two at a time. He kicked open the door of Room Twenty and went in. Trigger Moore lay on the floor by the window, his .30-30 beside him. He was dead, shot through the head.

Sam swung around and went back downstairs, dropping his gun into the holster. He stomped through the lobby, not so much as glancing at Stewart. Men had gathered around Rash's body— Charley Knowles and Abe Kahn and Doc Harvey and others.

"Charley, there's another hunk of carrion upstairs," Sam said, and started across the street to where Faraday still leaned against the front of the drugstore.

"Sam." Bill Barton, the liveryman, turned from the body and strode toward him. "Wait."

Ted Tull, the newspaper editor, ran to catch up with him. Sam waited in the middle of the street until they reached him, sensing that both men were hostile. He had faced death only minutes ago; his temper was ready to snap. He told himself that none of these men would have lifted a hand if he were the one lying in the street instead of Smoky Rash. The killers would have saddled up and ridden out of town, and that would have been the end of it.

They were in front of him then, red-faced Bill Barton and Ted Tull with the ink-stained fingers and the pasty complexion. Barton said: "We've got no quarrel with you about what just happened, but we do have a quarrel with you about jailing Monk Corley."

Tull nodded in agreement. "We were all shocked when it happened, but now that we've had time to think it over, we don't believe Monk is capable of killing a boy like Pete Nickels."

"Black Mike is the man responsible for what's happened," Barton added. "Not Monk. Or Rance Temple. Or Scotty Doane, neither. Why don't you arrest Black Mike and turn ...?"

This was all Sam could stand. He grabbed Barton by the shoulders and shook him till his teeth rattled. "You son-of-a-bitch!" Sam raged. "I just killed a man. I'd have been the one lying there in the dust instead of Rash if it hadn't been for Ben, and now you've got the gall to talk about turning those three killers loose."

He let go of Barton's shoulders as a series of fireworks spread a red pattern across his vision. He slapped Barton on one side of the face, rocking his big head, then slapped him on the other side. "I ought to knock you pizzle-end up. I was at Pete's funeral. So were you." He reached for Tull, but the editor jumped back out of reach.

"Sam!" Faraday called. "Stop it."

The fireworks died, and Sam knew this was the worst thing he could have done. But rage roared through him again when Tull screamed: "You don't know what public opinion is in this county, but you're going to find out! I'll have an editorial in the next issue that will singe your ears ..."

"And I'll bust hell out of you!" Sam shouted. "Don't you have any sense at all?"

"You'll see," Barton said hoarsely, one hand feeling of his cheeks. "You'll find out, bucko, who has the sense."

Faraday had hold of Sam's arm. "Come on," he said. Sam turned and started back toward the courthouse, his fury leaving him a little sick. He took the rifle from Faraday, realizing how wobbly the sheriff was.

"You've got to learn to take this kind of thing if you're going to be a lawman," Faraday said. "We'll have a hearing for our three prisoners before Judge Murray as soon as we can, but unless we find more evidence, we'd better be prepared to see them go free."

"Then we'll find more evidence," Sam said in a low voice. "I won't stand for Corley walking away from this."

"Tull was right about one thing," Faraday said. "Public opinion is more powerful than you think. Sometimes it forces the sheriff's office to do things that don't seem right, but the fact is no one can keep law and order when public opinion is against it as strong as it may be before this case is finished."

Sam was silent until they reached the courthouse. He would not argue with Faraday. He suspected that his father was the man who did the most to shape public opinion, and he could not change his father's attitude.

"Thanks for saving my life," Sam said. "I guess you figured it out a long time ago."

"I know how men like that think," Faraday said. "Now I'm going home and lie down if you can keep a tight rope on your temper."

"Yeah, I think I can," Sam said, and went into the sheriff's office.

He sat down at the desk, his hands fisting in front of him as he thought about what Faraday had said. Jonas Cassidy and the men who looked to him for leadership would not change their attitude until more evidence was found and that was not going to be easy.

XIX

For three days nothing happened, nothing that Sam could definitely put his finger on. Faraday grew a little weaker, a little paler, a little thinner, but he still was able to walk from his cabin to the sheriff's office and back to the cabin three times a day so Sam could get away for his meals. Sam knew, and he was sure that Faraday knew, that the time was not far distant when he could not make even that short walk.

Scotty Doane seemed to become a little more fearful each day, Rance Temple more sullen, and Monk Corley louder in his threats of what was going to happen to Sam and Scotty Doane and Ben Faraday when Jig Delaney came with the MC boys and got him out of jail. Sam still thought they'd come, but he had no idea when.

Something else was happening and this was the something that bothered Sam, although it was as elusive as smoke. Every time he went into the hotel dining room for a meal or the bar for a drink, it seemed to him that the townsmen turned their backs or walked away or simply stared at him as if he were a pariah who had committed some evil, unnamed crime. This treatment was entirely different from his reception the afternoon he had come in on the stage. Even Morry Jacks, the town drunk, looked the other way if they passed on the street. Maybe, he thought, he could expect this.

Cañon was a cow town, and he had arrested and was helping to hold in jail two of the biggest cowmen in the county. As soon as the townspeople had recovered from the shock of the murder, they had rallied behind Corley and Rance, claiming they could not have committed the crime.

Along with this hostile attitude was something that bothered Sam, something that he had not expected. It seemed to him that there was a strange tension that stemmed from waiting, a sort of expectancy as if these men were saying: *There's no hurry. We'll get to you in good time, Sam Cassidy, and we'll take care of you when we do.*

He mentioned this to Faraday when he returned to the sheriff's office after dinner on the third day, and he said: "I can't tell whether this is my imagination or not, Ben. Maybe I'm just boogery, waiting for Jig Delaney and his outfit to hit town."

Faraday nodded. "Maybe you are."

"It doesn't seem that men like Barton and Kahn and Tull would try to break Corley out of jail," Sam said. "I don't think they've got the guts to try."

"I don't think so, either," Faraday agreed, "but there's nothing we can do but wait and be ready for what happens. I know how you feel. Your nerves start getting tight as fiddle strings at a time like this, and all you can do is to keep from losing your head."

The sheriff started to get up, and then sat down again, his gaze on the doorway. Sam turned to see his father standing there. He was momentarily surprised, then he realized he had been expecting this.

"I don't want to intrude," Jonas said hesitantly, "but I've got something to say and I want to say it to both of you."

"Come in, Dad," Sam said. "Go ahead."

Jonas stepped into the office, walking gingerly as if he were on a slick floor and any minute might slip and fall on his face. He had his black derby in his hands and kept turning it so that the brim made a full circle in the short time it took him to walk from the doorway to the desk.

"I'm not backing up on anything I've said," Jonas began, "or changing sides or anything like that. I want you to understand it. If Monk or Rance or both of them did the killing, they should be punished. The point I've made all the time is that Kitty is a prejudiced witness. Scotty Doane might be trying to push the crime off on someone else. Monk claims he was playing poker with Jig Delaney that night. Now if you could prove he wasn't playing poker, that he was there at the sheep camp, then I would change my attitude."

Sam nodded and Faraday simply waited, both sensing this was a defense Jonas had to make to justify what he had said and done the last few days. By now he was sorry he had gone as far as he had, Sam thought, but he was sure his father would not admit it. Still, this was the first time he had known his father to back down or admit the possibility that he had been wrong.

"I've said this a thousand times in the last few days," Jonas went on. "I've said it in the hotel bar and in every saloon in town. Now I'm afraid I've sowed more seed than I intended. There's talk about lynching Black Mike because he's the one who's to blame for what's happened. If he hadn't moved his sheep ..." Jonas shrugged. "No sense going into that. The point is that my bank and every business in town depends on the cattlemen." He cleared his throat. "Well, I'm here because I don't believe in lynching. I understand something about law and order I did not understand a few days ago. If it breaks down and we have mob rule, my bank would be the first business place that would be looted." He cleared his throat again. "I wanted you to be warned about a lynching if Black Mike is still in town."

"Thanks," Faraday said coldly.

Jonas clapped his derby on his head. "Samuel, as far as I'm concerned, you can work at anything you want to. If you see your mother, ask her to come home." He swallowed, and with great effort added: "Kitty can come, too."

"I'll tell her," Sam said.

Jonas left them. Sam rolled a cigarette, not saying anything until he was sure his father was gone, then he said: "Ben, that's the first time in my life when Dad ever even hinted at the possibility he had been wrong about anything."

Faraday nodded. "You know what I think? He wants your mother back home so bad he'd help hang Monk Corley to get her."

"It might be," Sam said. "Neither Ma nor I ever bucked him before. He didn't know how to handle it when we did."

Faraday rose. "Don't rush over to see your ma. Jonas got himself between a rock and a hard place for the first time in his life. It tickles me to see him sweat." He walked to the door, then stopped and looked back. "He knows damned well that Corley did the killing and he's going to admit it before we're done."

He left then, and Sam settled down to a long, boring afternoon of waiting. He couldn't go on spending his afternoons this way. Sooner or later he'd have to find someone to spell him off so he could have a little time with Kitty and get away for a few hours at least from this miserable little town that did not deserve a lawman like Ben Faraday. Next time, he thought, it might get a man it did deserve.

That evening Tommy Riggs was late bringing supper to the prisoners. It was dusk, and Sam sensed at once that Tommy was so excited he could hardly control himself. As soon as the prisoners had their meals and Tommy was back in the sheriff's office, he said: "They're fixing to do it tonight. Real soon, too. Of course I just heard a little here and a little there, but it all adds up. Barton's the one that's leadin' 'em."

"They're fixing to do what?" Sam asked.

He thought he knew, if what his father had said was true, but he wanted to be sure. He waited, looking at the boy who seemed surprised that Sam didn't know.

"They've been talking about hanging Black Mike for three days," Tommy said. "He's in town. Came in for supplies and bought some stuff from Abe Kahn. Now they're going after him."

This made no sense at all. Hanging Black Mike Nickels had no relationship whatever to Monk Corley's guilt, but making sense was something fearful men were not capable of doing. They probably knew, as Faraday said Jonas Cassidy knew, that Monk Corley had killed Pete Nickels. Now, caught on the horns of a dilemma, they had to have a scapegoat, so they were striking at a man they had never liked, a man who had set into motion the chain of events that had culminated in Pete's murder.

"Tommy, run over to the sheriff's cabin and see if he feels like coming back," Sam said. "He can lie down on the cot. Tell him I've got to go to the Nickels house."

"You ain't gonna tell nobody what I said?" Tommy asked, suddenly scared. "Hoby is talking real big and tough, and he'd take it out on me if he knowed."

"I won't tell," Sam said.

He filled his pockets with shotgun shells and, taking the double-barreled gun from the rack, ran out of the courthouse. He took a back street to the Nickels house and went into it from the alley, calling: "Kitty! Ma!"

Lit lamps were in the kitchen and the dining room. He shut and barred the back door as both women ran into the kitchen. They stopped, surprised, and Kitty asked: "Has something happened?"

"It's going to," he said. "Is Black Mike here?"

"He left about half an hour ago," Mrs. Cassidy said.

"Did he go down Main Street?"

"No," Kitty answered. "Abe Kahn was ugly when Pa bought his supplies this afternoon. Some threats were made and he decided he'd better get back to the sheep camp. He's looking for another raid. Anyhow, he waited till it was pretty late and said he'd circle around and hit the road out of town a ways."

"Our trouble's going to happen right here," Sam said. "They're coming to lynch him. They won't believe me that he's not here, but I'm not going to let them in the house or they'll tear it apart. Hard to tell what would happen to both of you if they got inside. Both of you can shoot. You may have to before the night's over. Kitty, fetch all the guns you've got in the house and lay them out so we can use them. Ma, blow out the lamps. I'll watch from the front door. I don't think any man in town has guts to buck our guns when they know we've got them lined up and ready to shoot."

Kitty ran into the bedroom and came back with two rifles, a revolver, and a shotgun. She said as she laid them on the table: "One thing about Pa. He always believed in being prepared. Years go he said this might happen, that a sheepman living in a cattleman's country was bound to get into trouble."

"Then why did he start this in the first place?" Sam demanded. "Why wasn't he satisfied to stay where he was?"

For a moment Kitty didn't answer. He could not see her face in the near darkness. Then he heard her ask: "Sam, are you or Jonas or Monk Corley satisfied to stay where you are?"

"No," he admitted. "I guess any man has a right to grow."

"That's what Pa said. He claimed he had as much right to a part of the Public Domain as anyone else did." She ran into the bedroom and returned with half a dozen boxes of shells. "That's it."

"Good." When Sam's mother came into the front room, he said: "Pick out your weapon. I saw Dad this noon. He wants you to come back. He says Kitty can come, too."

She picked up a rifle and jacked a shell into the chamber, then she said: "He never could do even the simplest things for himself. All right, I'll go back, but he'll have to ask me. You tell him that."

"I'll tell him," Sam said.

Kitty, watching from an open window, said: "Here they come."

Sam picked up the shotgun. "If I can't bluff them, shoot to kill. An hour ago these men were your neighbors. Now they're animals making up a mob." Then he stepped outside and put his back to the wall and waited.

XX

The only noise the mob made as it came along the street was the scuffing of shoes in the dust. The light was so thin that Sam could not identify them, but he thought that the big man leading them was the liveryman, Bill Barton. Sam had no respect for these men. They gave each other courage, but not one of them would have been here if he'd come alone. Sam waited until they were in front of the house and the man in front opened the gate, the rusty hinges squeaking as loudly as ever. Black Mike still had not oiled them. Just as the man in front stepped into the Nickels yard, Sam cocked both barrels of the shotgun.

"Stop right there!" he called. "I've got a double-barreled shotgun in my hands. You're trespassing with the intention of breaking into this house and murdering the owner. If I shot the lot of you, I'd be doing my duty as deputy sheriff of this county."

They stopped, no one saying anything for more than a minute. Probably they were all armed, but it was hard to place his position in the near darkness, standing as he was against the wall of the house, so he was reasonably sure none of them would shoot. On the other hand, they were all in the open and they were very much aware of it.

Suddenly Doc Harvey laughed. He said: "That's the stuff, Sam.

I told them you were a better man than all of them put together. Now you boys go on home and forget it."

"We want Black Mike," Barton said.

"If he was here, he'd hold you off like I'm doing," Sam said, "but he's not here. Nobody is in the house but Kitty and my mother. They both have guns and they can shoot better than most of you, so just keep coming and the ones in front will be dead and the rest of you will be running."

"We don't believe Black Mike left the house!" a man yelled. "Let us take a look inside. If he's not there, we'll leave peaceably."

Sam wasn't sure, but he thought it was Ted Tull, the newspaperman. Sam said: "Oh no, you won't. I told you I'd kill the first man who comes up that walk. I can't see very good, but buckshot spreads pretty good, so some of you will get it. I wouldn't let you in if Black Mike was here, but I'm sure not going to with Kitty and my mother in the house."

"We don't believe Mike ..." Barton began.

"Abe," Sam called. "Abe Kahn, are you in the crowd?"

"Yeah, I'm here," the storekeeper said.

"Abe, Black Mike bought supplies this afternoon from you," Sam said. "I wasn't in the store when he was there, but Kitty tells me you and him had a little argument and you made some threats. That right?"

"Yeah, that's right," Kahn said reluctantly. "I told him my business had gone to hell the last few days and he was to blame for starting the talk about wanting more range and moving his sheep across the deadline and sending for Dale Sontag. I told him we was gonna get him."

"I guess that was why he decided to leave tonight," Sam said. "You know him well enough to be damned sure he wasn't scared, but he didn't want any more trouble. He was afraid the sheep camp might be raided again, so he decided to go back."

Still they stood there, afraid to rush the house and too proud to give up so easily. Exasperated, Sam said: "Ma, I guess they don't think you and Kitty are there with rifles. Take a shot at the ground in the front yard. If you get a little high and shoot Abe or Ted or Morry or any of the others, it will be all right because you are defending yourself and Kitty against a mob. Nobody can blame you for that."

Mrs. Cassidy's rifle cracked, a ribbon of powder flame flashing into the fading twilight. A man yelled in fright and started to run. It was probably Morry Jacks, Sam thought. It took very little to drain his whiskey courage out of him.

"You got rid of one of them," Sam said. "Kitty, see what you can do."

She fired from the other window. By this time most of them had had enough. They began moving away, and a moment later only Barton and two other men stood beside the gate. Doc Harvey had moved away from the others as if he wanted to let Sam know he had no part in this.

"Git," Sam said, his patience gone. "Barton, I'm going to give you just about five seconds. If you're still there, I'm coming down there."

"Go on home, Bill," Doc Harvey said. "This was a bad idea to start with just like I told you. Sam, I want to talk to you after these three brave men go home."

Barton wheeled through the gate and stomped away, cursing. The other two followed. Doc Harvey came up the path, calling: "Missus Cassidy, will you or Kitty light a lamp?"

He stopped just a step from the porch, waiting until the lamp was lit and the yellow finger of light spilled through the door. Sam, seeing him for the first time since the morning after the murder, was shocked. Doc Harvey was not an old man, but now he looked old. It seemed to Sam that he had aged twenty years in these few days since Sam and Ben Faraday had talked to him in front of Augie Pope's cabin.

For a moment Doc Harvey stared at Sam, but Sam remained out of the lamplight. The doctor was exactly like Jonas Cassidy. If he treated Rance Temple or one of his boys, or Monk Corley or an MC hand, he was paid and paid well. In the twenty-odd years that he had practiced medicine in Cañon, he had never spared himself, he had done good work, and he had prospered. He had lied that morning in front of Augie Pope's cabin simply because he had not wanted to upset the apple cart. He had lived with that lie since then, and, judging from his expression, it had not been easy. Sam guessed that he was finally being driven to tell the truth, but Sam had no intention of making it easy for him.

"Let's go into the house," Harvey said, and, without waiting for Sam, went past him into the front room.

For a moment he looked at Kitty. He said: "I brought you into the world, young woman. Some other doctor could have done it, but the fact is I was the one who did." He turned to Mrs. Cassidy. "I was with you when Sam was born. It wasn't an easy birth. For a while I thought we were going to lose the baby."

He stopped and pulled at his beard, and then said: "Kitty, find me some paper and a pen and a bottle of ink."

He sat down at the table and pushed back the boxes of ammunition and the guns. Kitty brought him the writing materials he had requested. He dipped the pen, then he looked up at Sam who stood in the doorway. He said: "You're tougher than anybody gave you credit for. We have enough lawyers in the county, but we don't have anybody else to take Ben's place when he dies, and I guess you know he doesn't have much longer."

He cleared his throat, still nervous and ill at ease, and started to write, then he stopped and tipped his head back and fixed his gaze on Sam's face again. "I don't know where you got your toughness. It sure wasn't from Jonas, so I guess it was from your mother. Now we'll see if you have some mercy and compassion to go along with your toughness. Can you forgive me for lying to you?"

Sam had not expected this. He hesitated, then he said: "It depends on whether you are going to tell the truth now."

"I am."

"And will you go to Dad with me?"

"I will."

Sam saw the strain in the doctor's face; he sensed the tension that gripped him, and for the first time he realized how hard it was for this man, respected and admired as few men were, to admit that he had lied.

"Yes, I can forgive you," Sam said, "but it would have been easier for Ben and me if you had told the truth in the first place."

"I know." Harvey stared at the paper before him. "If you live as long as I have, you'll learn that it seldom pays to bite the hand that feeds you. Ben Faraday is an unusual man in that regard. What I'm doing now will not pay me." His laugh was a harsh, humorless sound. "I've got religion. Maybe I found out that I'm not as afraid of Monk Corley and Jig Delaney and the rest of the big cattlemen as I thought I was."

He was silent then, the scratching of his pen the only sound in the room. Sam, looking at the top of his head with its pink, round spot where the hair had departed years ago, thought he hadn't given the real reason for his "getting religion." Sam had a hunch that Doc Harvey had finally come to grips with the problem exactly as his father had.

Jonas had said at noon that he knew something about law and order he had not known before, that if it broke down, his bank would be the first business place to be looted. Doc Harvey had no bank, but he owned property and he had a profitable practice. If Monk Corley could murder a boy like Pete Nickels and walk away from it a free man, there was no deterrent to keep someone who hated Doc Harvey from shooting him and walking away from it.

Sam was certain that his father wanted to change sides, he wanted to keep Monk Corley in jail to stand trial, but he had to have an excuse to save face when he made a turnabout like that. Sam hoped the doctor's testimony would be enough.

Harvey finished and put his pen down, then picked up the paper and handed it to Sam who read:

I swear before God this is the truth and I will so testify in court. On the morning following the murder of Pete Nickels I was at Augie Pope's cabin waiting for the birth of the Pope baby. Monk Corley, Rance Temple, and Scotty Doane rode by. They were going toward Cañon and had come from the direction of the sheep camp. They stopped for a cup of coffee. Corley bragged about shooting a big part of the band of sheep belonging to Black Mike Nickels.

Dr. Enos Harvey

Sam handed the paper to his mother who read what Harvey had written, then she gave it to Kitty who read it and passed it back to Sam.

"All right, Doc," Sam said. "We'll go see Dad. Kitty, I don't think you and Ma will have any more trouble, but keep the house locked anyhow and one of you stay up."

Kitty nodded, then she ran to him and hugged him. "They're going to try to get Corley out of jail, aren't they?"

"They'll try," Sam said.

Harvey was on his feet, still nervous and tense. Now he looked at Sam, plainly uncertain, and suddenly seemed to make up his mind. He said: "They're going to try tonight. About daylight, I think. You'll have a dozen men to fight. The MC crew and the Temple boys and anybody else they can get."

Sam didn't ask how the doctor knew. The important thing was that Harvey had told him. He didn't doubt the accuracy of the information for a moment. He said curtly—"Then we'd better get a move on."—and left the house, the doctor a step behind.

XXI

The Cassidy house was dark when Sam and Doc Harvey reached it. Sam wondered about that because his father habitually spent his evenings at home. He paused on the sidewalk, thinking Jonas wasn't here, but Harvey went on up the path to the front door and yanked on the bell pull.

"Who is it?" Jonas called.

"Me," Harvey answered. "Doc. Sam's with me."

"Come in," Jonas said. "I'll light a lamp."

Sam followed Doc Harvey, wondering why his father had been sitting in the darkness. The lamp in the front room was lit now, and when Sam stepped through the hall doorway, he decided his father couldn't bear to look at the mess.

And it was indeed a mess. The floor and furniture were gray with dust that had blown in through the open windows. Newspapers and books were haphazardly on the chairs, the orange love seat, and the oak table. Even the lamp chimney needed cleaning. Jonas Cassidy was no perfectionist when it came to keeping house. Sam wondered what the kitchen was like. But Jonas was not a man to apologize for anything, not even his appearance. His shirt was dirty, his hair disheveled, but he had only one thought. The instant he saw Sam, he demanded: "Did you ask your mother if she would come home?"

Sam nodded. "She'll come, but you'll have to ask her."

Jonas groaned. "I don't want to do that." He wiped a hand across his face, the stubble making a sandpapery sound, then he added: "But I guess I'll have to."

"Show him my statement," Harvey said. "We're going to be busy, Jonas, trying to undo the damage we've both done. Me for not speaking up, and you for going around lighting a lot of little fires that damned near started a big one."

Jonas took the paper from Sam, asking: "What kind of a big one?"

Harvey told him about the lynch mob, adding: "There wasn't any sense to it, but people who are scared long enough don't have much sense. The town boys are plenty scared of Jig Delaney. He's been getting madder by the minute. He says we're all to blame for Monk being in jail, so he's fixing to burn the town. I guess Barton and Kahn and the rest figured that Delaney might be satisfied if they strung up Black Mike, and helped break Monk out of jail."

Jonas stared at Harvey and shook his head. "Jig wouldn't burn the town."

"Oh, come on, Jonas," Harvey said. "You kept saying Monk didn't murder Pete Nickels, but he did. We're going to talk the town boys out of helping Delaney, so he'll try to burn the town, all right, especially if they've all been drinking, which they probably have."

Jonas thought about it a moment, then glanced at the paper, and stiffened. "Well, if you'd told the truth ..."

"You knew I lied," Harvey said angrily. "What's more, you were lying to yourself about Monk. You didn't want your nice little business situation upset, but it's going to be. If you and I don't get Barton and Kahn and the rest of our town friends straightened out so Sam gets some help, we'll lose everything."

Jonas handed the sheet of paper back to Sam. "I never have done any fighting."

"Neither have I," Harvey said, "but we're starting tonight. We've been on the wrong side, letting Monk Corley run everything the way we have. You've got a fighting son and you'd better back him. If you don't, you'll have Monk Corley's law from now on and you're not going to like that."

"All right," Jonas said as he blew out the light. "Let's get at it. I know one thing. I don't want to live this way."

"You go back to the courthouse, Sam," the doctor said. "We're going to the hotel bar. I figure we'll find our brave mob drowning their disappointment. Maybe we won't shoot straight, but I can promise you we will shoot. I think you and Ben can hold them off."

"Sure we can," Sam said.

As he left the house and turned toward the courthouse, he told himself he was lying. He wasn't at all sure they could hold off Delaney's men, as sick as Faraday was. He looked for no effective help from the townsmen, so it boiled down, the way he saw it, to how many men Jig Delaney brought to town. He locked the front door of the courthouse and went on back to the sheriff's office. A lit lamp was on the desk. He stepped into the side room and found Faraday, lying on the cot. He said: "The talk is that Delaney is making his try tonight. Can you stay here?"

"I'll stay here," Faraday said.

Sam told him what had happened, and added: "A kind of a miracle, I guess, Doc deciding to tell the truth and Dad going with him to help fight Delaney."

"No miracle," Faraday said. "When a man like Doc Harvey gets religion as you put it, you can depend on one thing. He's changed his mind about where his best interest lies. Chances are he's decided we're going to win. Anyhow, it's like he told Jonas. He don't want Corley law, and if we lose tonight, that's what they'll have. It's the same with your dad except that he wants your ma back, too, and he knows he won't get her back if he don't start being part of a man."

"I guess," Sam said, and turned away.

"Sam," Faraday said.

He looked back. "What is it, Ben?"

"No use fooling ourselves," Faraday said. "I'm at the end of the string. I never bucked Monk Corley before, but he always knew he couldn't buffalo me, so in a way I kind of kept him in line. When I'm gone, you're the only one who can do it, so you've got to keep on wearing that star."

"I guess I will," Sam said. "For a while."

He went back into the office and took a Winchester from the gun rack. Then, carrying both the rifle and shotgun, he returned to the front door and sat down on the floor by a window. He didn't know what Delaney and his men would do. Try to break in the door with a battering ram, probably. The back door was as solid as this one and was kept locked except during some kind of an emergency. Suddenly it occurred to him that the janitor might have been bribed to unlock it, so he checked it. He found it locked, but as he returned to the front door, the thought occurred to him that if Delaney divided his men into two parties and battered both doors in, he was whipped. For the first time he faced the future alone. Ben Faraday might live for days, but just as he had said, he'd come to the end of his string. The chances were good he'd never get off that cot.

The hours dragged by. Once in a while Sam would drop off and nod and wake up. The moon rose, bathing the courthouse block with its yellow light, then, not long before dawn, he heard someone running toward the front door.

"Who is it?" Sam called.

"Mike Nickels," was the answer. "Let me in."

Sam unlocked the front door and Black Mike stumbled in, blowing hard. Sam locked the door and turned. "I thought ..."

"I thought, too," Black Mike said, "and what I thought was that right here was where the trouble would be, not at the sheep camp, so I left the wagon at Augie Pope's cabin and rode back." He stopped and took a long breath. "It's a good thing I done it, too. They're on their way, and from the sound of the horses, Delaney must have an army."

XXII

Sam unlocked the door and stepped outside to listen. Horses were coming, all right, but he could not tell how many or how far away they were. He glanced toward the business block, wondering what had happened to the help he was supposed to get from his father and Doc Harvey and the rest of the townsmen. He closed and locked the door again, thinking sourly that it was up to him and Black Mike and Ben Faraday, who was close to death. He should have known all the time it would be this way.

"What'll they do, Mike?" Sam asked.

"Bust the door down," Black Mike answered. "They'll guess it'll be locked, so they'll show up with a log and batter the door in. They'll unlock the cell and take Corley and Temple out, and they'll murder Scotty Doane, if we let 'em."

"That's about the way I figured it," Sam said. "I think we can hold them at this door, but if they take a whack at both of them, we've got big trouble."

"I'd better take the other door," Black Mike said. "It'll be daylight in a little bit, and the moon will be up till then. The doors ain't gonna give way at the first crack, so one of us standing at a window can give 'em hell."

Sam nodded, not wanting it that way, but deciding it was the best defense. If he had two more men ... He shrugged. Wishes were one thing. Reality was something else.

"How about Dale Sontag?" Sam asked, suddenly remembering the Utah sheepman Black Mike had sent for. "You still figuring on him coming?"

"Hell no," Mike snapped. "I know when I've had enough trouble."

That was one worry out of the way. Right now Delaney and his men were enough to worry about. "Any way you look at it," Sam said, "what Delaney is doing doesn't make sense. Even if Corley gets out of jail, the murder charge will still be against him."

"Sure, but he can beat it," Black Mike said. "You're forgetting something. Ben Faraday has been sheriff of this county a long time. I never liked him 'cause he's been a cowman right along same as Corley, but it's a fact that Corley never gave him an order. This time Corley could have handled him if you hadn't come home when you did, so you can figure they won't leave you alive. The next sheriff will take Corley's orders, and he'll dismiss the case for lack of evidence."

Sam turned back to the window, a little sick at the stomach. It would happen just about the way Black Mike had said. He picked up his rifle and knocked glass from the window, then stood motionlessly, listening. He didn't hear the horses now. For a moment he wondered if Delaney and his men had turned back and dismissed the thought at once. They'd had a reason for stopping. But what was it? He had assumed they would ride into town at a gallop, shooting at anything and everything. That was Jig Delaney's way, and it was typical of the MC crew that usually hit town for a spree on Saturday afternoons. Not that the cowboys intended to hurt anybody, but if you wanted to live, you ducked for cover. Now the silence bothered Sam.

Black Mike had moved along the hall to the other door. Sam, the Winchester in his hands, stood close to the broken window, listening and staring at the weed-covered yard. They were out there, he thought, somewhere in the shadows, perhaps across the street. Maybe they wouldn't try to batter down the door. They might stay on the other side of the street and rake the courthouse with rifle fire until they had cut down the defenders, then rush it and break Corley out of jail. Or they might not try the doors at all. There were windows on the first floor that they could sneak up to and not be seen from here or from the other end of the hall where Black Mike stood. They could crawl through one of the windows and ...

Then they came, darting out of the shadows from around the corner of the building. There were eight or ten of them. He had no time to count. They carried a log, and before he could cock and fire the rifle, they had smashed at the locked door. It groaned and shivered, but it withstood that first smashing attack.

Sam shot one man, Slim Goble he thought, and saw him spin away and fall. He realized the rifle was the wrong weapon; he dropped it and grabbed the shotgun and let go with a load of buckshot. One man screamed and fell and started to crawl back toward the corner of the courthouse. Sam triggered another blast as the log rammed against the door a second time. Again it shuddered and splintered, but at least one hinge still held. He had no way of knowing if he had hit any of them that time or not. He was shooting at an angle and they were close to the door.

He threw the shotgun down and drew his Colt as the log slammed home a third time. That did it. The door crashed open and the MC men poured into the hall just as Black Mike, standing at the far end, opened fire. The invaders were caught in a tight bunch, with Sam shooting from the side and Black Mike from the other end of the hall. The firing was too hot for them. As they broke and ran, the townsmen rushed into the street and raced across the yard in front of the courthouse.

In the moonlight Sam recognized his father and Doc Harvey leading the charge. They were yelling and shooting and making enough racket for a regiment. The cowboys must have thought it was a regiment. The ones who were able to run didn't linger to see.

Sam reloaded his revolver and moved to the doorway. Apparently Abe Kahn had opened up the Mercantile and passed rifles out to the townsmen. They were all armed. Jonas Cassidy had never used a rifle, at least not in Sam's memory, and he probably wasn't hitting anything now, but at least he was doing his share of the shooting.

Suddenly Sam was aware that he had not seen anything of Black Mike, and he hadn't heard him for a while. He ran back along the hall and found the sheepman sprawled on his back in front of the door he had been guarding. Sam picked up his wrist and felt of his pulse. It was strong and regular. He must have been knocked cold, maybe from a gun barrel. That meant only one thing. Jig Delaney or one or more of his men were inside the building.

Sam wheeled toward the sheriff's office, his revolver in his hand. He heard a shot and began to run. He reached the door and saw Ben Faraday sprawled on the floor, his .45 inches from an outstretched hand. The corridor door was closing. Sam lunged across the office and yanked the door open. Jig Delaney had the key ring in his hand and was trying to fit a key into the lock of the door to the big cell that held Corley and Temple.

Monk Corley yelled a warning. Delaney whirled, pulling his gun as he turned. Sam shot him through the chest, shot him as coldly and mercilessly as he would have killed a mad dog. The heavy slug from the .45 knocked Delaney off his feet. He spilled full length on the floor, then rolled over and reached for the gun he had dropped. He gripped it, his lips pulled away from his teeth in a grimace of agony, and then Sam shot him again. His head fell, rapping against the floor.

Sam walked to him and rolled him over. He picked up the gun and faced Corley and Temple who were standing motionlessly, staring at Sam as if they expected him to kill both of them.

"He's dead, Monk," Sam said. "I'll leave him right there for you to look at. You don't deserve the loyalty you got from him. You'll have a hearing before Judge Murray and you'll be held for trial and you're going to hang. I hope Pete's waiting for you in hell and blackballs you the minute you walk in."

He stomped out of the jail and, picking up Ben Faraday's body, carried him to the cot and laid him down. He was shocked at how much the sheriff had wasted away. He seemed no heavier than a child. He knew Faraday had been eating very little and was losing weight, but he had not realized how far it had gone. For a moment Sam stood looking down at the body, thinking Faraday must have heard Delaney come in and had tried to stop him. At least he had got to his feet and had been able to walk into the office from the side room. The MC foreman had shot him and had gone on back into the jail.

Sam was surprised at his own feelings. He was not sorry this had happened. He knew Faraday would have preferred to die in the manner he had rather than linger in bed for days and be waited on hand and foot. There was a time to be born, to live and fight for what you believe in, and to die, and this was the way he would have wanted it. One thing was sure. In these last few days Sam had learned a great deal from Ben Faraday about being a man.

When he went back into the hall, he found the townsmen milling around aimlessly, as excited as a bunch of boys who had just won a fight with another bunch of boys across town. Someone had lit a bracket lamp. Black Mike was on his feet, holding his head. When he saw Sam, he asked: "Who was it, Delaney?"

"That's right," Sam answered. "He shot and killed Ben."

Black Mike swore, and said: "He must have got in through a window. With all the shooting, I didn't hear him. All I remember was that I was firing away at them bastards when they came piling through the door and then I got it. It was a pretty tricky idea, too. He figured we'd be watching the crowd, so he'd slip into the jail, get Corley and Temple out, and give 'em guns."

"It might have worked if Ben hadn't taken a hand," Sam said.

Jonas made his way through the crowd. When he reached Sam,

he said: "We didn't expect them to maneuver this way. We were ready for them on both sides of the street. Doc said they wouldn't figure on us giving them any trouble and they'd ride in from the other direction."

"We'd have fixed 'em, too," Bill Barton said as if this had been his side all along. "Yes, sir, we'd have emptied some saddles, all right."

"We chased 'em to hell and gone," Morry Jacks said, speaking up, big and proud. "Did you see the way we ran 'em off, Sam?"

"I saw it," Sam said, and turned away before his temper snapped and he twisted a few necks.

He noticed that Jonas and Black Mike were facing each other, neither knowing quite what to say, then Black Mike said: "Aw, hell, Jonas, we might as well shake hands. Our kids are gonna get married no matter what we do."

"That's right," Jonas said. "No use bucking it." He held out his hand and Black Mike took it, then Jonas added: "If you'll come into the bank, we'll talk about a loan. That is, if you want to replace your sheep that were killed. That's another thing. Everything's going to be different now whether I like it or not."

"I guess it will," Black Mike said with forced heartiness. "Sure, I'll drop into the bank after I catch up on my sleep."

They would never like each other, Sam thought, but at least they'd be on speaking terms. Jonas Cassidy had learned something about being a decent person, although he might never be a man in the sense Ben Faraday had been.

"Let's go talk to a couple of women who are waiting for us," Sam said, and dropped a hand on Jonas' shoulder.

Jonas grinned a little. He did not jerk away as he had in the past when Sam touched him. He nodded and said: "I've eaten more damned crow the last few days, and I'm not done yet."

They went down the hall and out of the courthouse into the early morning light. Some of the men were helping Doc Harvey with the wounded cowboys, and Charley Knowles and Abe Kahn were carrying Slim Goble's body to the back room of the drugstore. Suddenly Sam realized that his father was running toward the Nickels house. This, Sam thought, was the first time he had ever seen any man run toward another meal of crow, least of all Jonas Cassidy.

THE END

ABOUT THE AUTHOR

Wayne D. Overholser won three Spur Awards from the Western Writers of America and has a long list of fine Western titles to his credit. He was born in Pomeroy, Washington, and attended the University of Montana, the University of Oregon, and the University of Southern California before becoming a public schoolteacher and principal in various Oregon communities. He began writing for Western pulp magazines in 1936 and within a couple of years was a regular contributor to Street & Smith's *Western Story Magazine* and Fiction House's *Lariat Story Magazine*. *Buckaroo's Code* (1947) was his first Western novel and remains one of his best. In the 1950s and 1960s, having retired from academic work to concentrate on writing, he would publish as many as four books a year under his own name or a pseudonym, most prominently as Joseph Wayne. *The Violent Land* (1954), *The Lone Deputy* (1957), *The Bitter Night* (1961), and *Riders of the Sundowns* (1997) are among the finest of the Overholser titles. *Bunch Grass* (1955) and *Land of Promises* (1962) are among the best Joseph Wayne titles, and *Law Man* (1953) is a most rewarding novel under the Lee Leighton pseudonym.

Overholser's Western novels, whatever the byline, are based on a solid knowledge of the history and customs of the nineteenth-century West, particularly when set in his two favorite Western states, Oregon and Colorado. Many of his novels are first-person narratives, a technique that tends to bring an added dimension of vividness to the frontier experiences of his narrators and frequently, as in *Cast a Long Shadow* (1957) filmed as *Cast A Long Shadow* (United Artists, 1959), the female characters one encounters are among the most memorable. He wrote his numerous novels with a consistent skill and an uncommon sensitivity to the depths of human character. Almost invariably, his stories weave a spell of their own with their scenes and images of social and economic forces often in conflict and the diverse ways of life and personalities that made the American Western frontier so unique a time and place in human history.